'Hey, Abbey..

'Let's see what the

'*You* were driving to

It was the same
from years ago. '*You* are walking too fast,
Ryan Henry. Wait for me!'

And he always had.

'You want to have me arrested?' Ryan's stern
face quirked into a smile. 'Hey, Abbey, I'm a
doctor and I might just be useful here. Let me
examine you before you have me hauled away
in handcuffs.'

Dear Reader

Far North Queensland and Australia's Great Barrier Reef combine to make one of the best, most romantic, most exotic and just plain fabulous holiday destinations in the world. Just ask me! My husband, my children and I love it. After every visit I return to my desk sandy, sunburned and gloriously happy. I'm ready to write more romances, but there's always a trace of 'I wish I could have stayed longer'.

This year, as we were waiting in Cairns airport for our flight south and back to work, a honeymoon couple arrived on the inward flight. They were obviously very much in love, they were weighed down with beach gear—and he was just gorgeous! So all the way south I sat and scowled. What if I hijacked her honeymoon…?

And the lovely thing about being a romance author is— that I just did! And I hope you enjoy it.

Marion Lennox

HIJACKED HONEYMOON

BY
MARION LENNOX

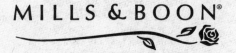

MILLS & BOON®

First published in Great Britain 1998
Harlequin Mills & Boon Limited,
Eton House, 18-24 Paradise Road, Richmond, Surrey TW9 1SR

© Marion Lennox 1998

ISBN 0 263 81072 0

Set in Times Roman 10 on 10½ pt.
03-9808-55563-D

Printed and bound in Norway
by AiT Trondheim AS, Trondheim

CHAPTER ONE

SAPPHIRE COVE, Australia, was definitely the loveliest place in the world for a honeymoon.

Pity about the bride.

Dr Ryan Henry eased his foot from the accelerator and gazed across the headland. What he saw was magic.

The sea below was the sapphire blue that gave the town its name. A yacht with white sail and crimson spinnaker stood out against the distant islands. The wind was warm and laced with salt and sunshine, and tropical growth surged between coconut palms all along the roadside.

Magic, indeed.

His mother hadn't thought so.

'Sapphire Cove is the end of the earth,' Ryan's mother had told him when she'd taken him to the States seventeen years ago. Ryan had been fifteen years old and his parents' marriage had collapsed. 'Don't ever let your father talk you into coming back.'

His father had never tried, and Australia was no longer part of Ryan's life. But the idea of Far North Queensland for a honeymoon appealed to Felicity, and the fact that Ryan hadn't seen his father for seventeen years intrigued his intended bride.

'Ryan, I didn't know you still had Australian citizenship. Hey, I have a conference in Hawaii in November. What if we meet in Australia straight afterwards? We can marry and honeymoon there, and maybe you can visit your father before I arrive.'

'We should arrive there together,' Ryan insisted. 'If I make my flight the day after your conference ends…'

Felicity arched her beautifully pencilled eyebrows and decided to humour him. Well, why not? Ryan Henry was certainly worth humouring. Tall, dark and drop-dead handsome, as well as being one of the country's most promising young surgeons, Ryan was a hunk in any woman's eyes.

'Scared of meeting your father on your own, then?' she teased. 'OK, Ryan, I'll come with you.'

But she hadn't. Ryan might have known she wouldn't. Emotional family reunions weren't Felicity's scene. Ryan had landed in Cairns this morning to be met by a message from Felicity. She was still in Hawaii.

'There's a post-conference meeting it's imperative I attend. Ryan, these people are *so important* career-wise. I'll join you when I can. Go on to Sapphire Cove and I'll meet you there.'

Yeah, great...

'Damn you, Felicity,' Ryan said savagely. The beauty of his home town faded in the face of his anger, and he shoved his foot on the pedal with more force than it deserved.

Mistake.

A bicycle flew out from a gravel side road straight across his path. Ryan hit the brakes hard, but he couldn't stop in time.

The bicycle ended up right beneath his car.

The world stopped.

There are some moments so awful that to replay them in memory or to try and describe them is unbearable. This was one of those moments.

For two seconds Ryan sat, stunned and frozen, while the sound of metal against metal faded to nothing. It seemed a lifetime that he sat there. In fact, it was two whole seconds.

Then he was out of the car and launching himself around the front of the bonnet to find the unimaginable horror that lay beneath.

There was a bike—or what had been a bike. A tangled heap of metal was buckled right under his car. For one awful moment Ryan thought the rider must be there too— beneath the twisted bike.

He wasn't. No. *She* wasn't. Dear God...

The rider—a girl—was crumpled and motionless on the verge of the road. She'd been thrown clear.

She was…dead?

As white as a ghost himself, somehow Ryan moved to see, and as he did the girl stirred and moaned.

The moan was a tiny sound. Her stirring was a tiny movement. But it was enough to shove Ryan back into medical mode—to lift him out of the nightmare a little, back to a mental framework where he'd been trained to cope. A medical emergency.

'Don't move,' he snapped urgently, and knelt down beside her on the gravel. His strong hands moved swiftly to press the girl back on the verge to stop her from rising. If her spine was fractured…. Or if she had head injuries…

He removed her bike helmet gently, half-afraid of what he might find. To his relief, the short, dark curls were unbloodied. Then he put all the authority he could muster into his voice in a vain attempt to override his shock. 'Don't try to move.'

Silence. The girl did as he ordered and lay absolutely still. Or maybe that initial movement had been his imagination.

At least she was breathing. Ryan ran his hands over her body to check her, his eyes taking her in. The girl's eyes were closed. She was young but not a child—maybe twenty or so. Slight. Five feet four or five. Black curly hair, close-cropped and shining. Finely boned with a wide, generous mouth and a neat little nose. In other circumstances she might be described as lovely. Very lovely. Wearing shorts and a T-shirt that said NO FEAR.

The slogan wasn't appropriate. Ryan was so fearful he could hardly breathe himself.

There wasn't a vestige of colour on the girl's face. She had a faint smattering of freckles across her nose and they only made her lack of colour look worse.

He had to see what damage there was. But to turn her…

'Do you think I might move just a bit?' a voice said cautiously. 'There's gravel sticking into my cheek.'

Ryan practically yelped.

Then he grinned, relief washing over him like a tidal wave. No brain damage here, then.

There were other sorts of damage.

'Wait a bit...'

'I think my spine's intact, if that's what you're worried about.' Still with her eyes closed and still motionless, the girl's voice seemed somehow disembodied. 'I can feel everything.'

The girl's voice wasn't as sure now as it had first sounded. It held a distinct tremble. And Ryan found himself putting medical imperatives aside and moving to touch her face. To comfort her.

'Hey. It's OK.' He stroked the soft, black curls as one might have reassured a frightened child. 'You're OK. I'm a doctor. You'll be fine.'

She opened her eyes at that, and stared straight up at him.

And he knew her.

Ryan Henry would have known those eyes anywhere. They'd taunted him as a child. Haunted him for years.

Abbey Rhodes had been eleven years old when he'd left Sapphire Cove. She was four years younger than he and his mother had hated her. 'White Trash' his mother had termed Abbey, and when she'd seen Abbey, trailing home alongside Ryan, she'd let loose with both barrels.

'Ryan, that child's mother's not married. Worse, she never has been married. She's poor as a church mouse and scrubs floors for a living. If that woman thinks you're going to waste time talking to her child... Well, that's why we're leaving, Ryan. This whole place has no class at all.'

Sapphire Cove didn't have 'class', Ryan acknowledged, and it was one of the things he remembered about Australia with affection. The Abbeys of the town, the poor, the immigrants, the local Koori kids whose parents thought houses were a waste of time—and Celia Henry's son—were all treated exactly the same by the locals. And, despite what Celia thought, Abbey had definitely regarded herself as the equal of Ryan. Or better.

'If you're going to be a world-famous doctor then so am I,' she'd declared, puffing out her eleven-year-old chest and snapping imaginary braces. 'I'm just as good as you, Ryan Henry, even if my mum does think your mum's snooty.'

Abbey's mother had house-cleaned for Celia Henry and, for a while, Abbey had followed Ryan around like a devoted little shadow. That was, until Celia had put an end to it for ever by moving Ryan away.

And all Ryan remembered of Abbey were her eyes. Her fabulous eyes...

Vivid blue. Direct. Honest. And clear as two big pools of water from the sapphire ocean.

Gorgeous!

They'd changed, though.

Ryan had assessed the slim girl lying on the road as being twenty or so. Well, if his figuring was right Abbey had to be more like twenty-seven or -eight now. And her eyes told him he was right, even if his arithmetic couldn't. Abbey's eyes were lined—creased from accustomed laughter. And from something else. Suffering?

'Well, I never...' Abbey managed, staring up at the man kneeling over her. 'It's Ryan Henry...'

It was a pain-filled whisper and it brought Ryan up with a jolt. She'd recognised him, too—but, damn, he was a doctor and she was injured.

'Hey, Abbey...' He touched her curls again and they were warm and soft to touch. 'Yeah, it's Ryan. But let's see what the damage is.'

'*You* were driving too fast.'

It was the same voice he remembered from years ago. '*You* are walking too fast, Ryan Henry. Wait for me!'

And he always had.

'You want to have me arrested?' Ryan's stern face quirked into a smile. 'Hey, Abbey, I'm a doctor and I might just be useful here. Let me examine you before you have me hauled away in handcuffs.'

'I think...' Abbey cautiously raised her head a little and winced in distress as Ryan helped her into a sitting position.

There was still pain in her voice. 'I think there's gravel stuck in my cheek.'

'There is.' Ryan looked at her face and he hardly saw the gravel rash. Abbey had had the promise of beauty when she was eleven. The promise had been fulfilled, and more. 'It's not too bad, though. It'll scrub out and shouldn't scar. What else hurts, Abbey?'

'My leg. Yikes, my leg…' Abbey grimaced. Ryan's arm was around her shoulders now and she found herself putting her face against the soft linen of his shirt. Finding comfort in the solidness of him.

As she'd found comfort in his company all those years ago.

She peered out from the folds of his shirt, along the line of her leg. 'Ryan, it's dislocated,' she whispered. 'Just look. The patella's way out of line.'

'The patella's way out of line…'

That wasn't what a non-medical person would say. They'd have said the leg was broken or that it looked funny, with the kneecap sitting out of line with the rest of the leg.

Had Abbey done nursing, then? Ryan wondered briefly. The Abbey he remembered would have made a good nurse. Cheerful and bouncy and never one to let life's knocks get her down.

'Let me see.'

Making sure she was able to sit unaided, Ryan shifted so he could examine her leg. One look told him it was out of position. Ryan's hands moved gently down over the injured limb and he knew she was right. It was at least dislocated. She'd be lucky if there wasn't a break as well.

He looked up at her face again and swore as he saw the deep pain in her eyes.

'You need morphine,' he said. 'I'm sorry, Abbey, but I don't have anything with me. We're just going to have to get you to the hospital as fast as we can.'

'Let me be,' she said weakly, and tried to bend over to put her hands on her leg. 'I'll try and get it back in…'

'*You*!' Ryan caught her hands and held them. 'Abbey, you can't...'

Abbey bit her lip, closed her eyes and curled her fingers into fists within Ryan's hold. For all her strength, the pain in her leg was building to the stage where she couldn't bear it. 'Ryan, let me try. I must...'

'But... I don't understand.' Ryan's grip on her hands tightened. 'Are you the district nurse? Doing house calls on your bicycle?'

'Close enough.' Abbey opened her eyes again then and met his look with a touch of defiance. 'I knew you didn't believe me all those years ago, Ryan Henry. I told you what I was going to be. I'm the local doctor.'

'You're the...'

'Look, I hate to be rude,' Abbey said wearily, 'but let's get my leg back to a straight line and catch up on career paths later, shall we?'

Abbey couldn't. Ryan didn't let her make the attempt, but a comprehensive examination of Abbey's leg told him he couldn't do it either. Not without a really hefty dose of morphine and sedative to relax her. The patella had twisted way out of position. She'd been incredibly lucky that the leg hadn't snapped.

'There's morphine in my bag,' Abbey told him. Abbey's bag, by some miracle, was hardly damaged. Ryan retrieved it by simply reversing the car off the bicycle. At least there was something he could do then. Ryan injected sub-cutaneous morphine into Abbey's thigh, considered trying to manipulate the leg then and there and decided against it. He wanted an X-ray first. To try and manipulate it and then discover that there was a break...

He splinted the leg as best he could with crêpe bandages and newspapers he had in the car, and then gathered her carefully into his arms.

Abbey hardly spoke as he worked. All the energy seemed to have gone out of her, and Ryan found himself growing increasingly worried about just how hard she'd hit her head.

'Thank you, Ryan,' she whispered. She put her arms unselfconsciously around his neck to help him lift her, and the feel of her made Ryan feel distinctly strange.

'My pleasure.' Ryan winced as he heard himself say it. Inane. That was how he felt. Young and gauche. Looking down at this slip of a girl was like looking at his childhood all over again.

It made him remember with a vengeance the things he had once loved. Memories came flooding back. The things and the people his mother had torn him from.

Abbey...

'Come on,' he said in a voice rougher than he'd intended. 'Let's get you to the hospital. I assume there's a hospital in this place now. Do you have another doctor who can patch you up?'

'We do have a hospital, but I'm afraid it's a case of "Physician, heal thyself",' she quoted wryly.

Ryan didn't respond. He steadied himself, made sure his grip was sure and the splint was supported by his arm and then lifted her into his arms and across to the car. She was a featherweight. She put her arms around his neck in a subconscious gesture of trust that made him feel even more odd.

'It's me, me or me,' Abbey added shakily as he set her down. 'Or—alternatively—me.'

Ryan gave himself a mental shake. What was it about this girl that was making emotions and memories he'd forgotten flood right back?

'Well, you can't put your own leg back into place,' he said brusquely.

'I probably can,' Abbey said thoughtfully. 'I don't think anything's broken. Let's get me X-rayed and then we'll see.'

'You have to be joking.'

'No.' Abbey perched on the car's back seat as Ryan lowered her. Then, as Ryan held her leg steady, she hauled herself backwards so that her leg was stretched out straight on the seat. Her voice still wobbled but there was a trace of defiance in the tone. Like—'Don't mess with me. I can handle myself!'

'I stitched up my gashed arm last year,' she told him. 'Ten stitches, all by myself. I don't see that this is any worse. Look, would you mind if we made a house call on the way to the hospital?' She took a deep breath. The morphine was beginning to cut in and the agony was receding.

'A house call...'

'I was on my way to see a patient,' Abbey told him. Her voice was growing stronger by the minute and Ryan frowned in disbelief. This was one tough lady and she was recovering fast from the shock.

'You were going on a house call on a bicycle?'

'Well, why not?' Abbey settled against the squabs of Ryan's luxury car and gave a sigh of relief. Once again, there was defiance in her voice. 'It's a gorgeous Sunday afternoon. I don't have anyone really sick in hospital. Mrs Miller's a non-urgent case and using my bicycle saves petrol.'

'Abbey...' This was getting crazier by the minute. Ryan climbed behind the wheel and looked over his shoulder at the girl on the back seat. There was blood on her face and her colour was still sickly. The 'No Fear' on her T-shirt looked crazy. Defiant. Like she was. Apart from the life creases around her eyes, she looked about ten. 'You're not really suggesting we do a house call before we take you to hospital?'

'I'd like to do it while the morphine's still working,' Abbey said seriously. 'I've been thinking. At a guess, I'm going to find it hard to get around for a day or two now, and Marg Miller wants to see me.'

'What about?' Ryan shook his head in bewilderment. 'You said it wasn't urgent.'

'She has an ulcer on her leg that needs dressing.'

'Surely you have a district nurse who can do that? Or are you the sole medical provider for the whole district?'

'We have district nurses,' Abbey said defensively. 'Three of them. But Marg wants to see *me*.'

'But not urgently.'

'No,' Abbey said thoughtfully. 'But there's something wrong. Not just the ulcer. She wouldn't have asked me to come unless she was worried. There's something troubling her.'

Ryan sighed. His hands gripped the wheel tightly.

Good grief! It had been a long flight from New York and he'd worked at full pace right up to the minute he'd left. He'd just had the fright of his life—he'd thought he'd killed her—and now Abbey was suggesting that they go and dress an ulcer that could probably be dressed by the nurse at any time over the next couple of days.

'No,' he said in a voice that was implacable. Head-of-surgical-team implacable. 'If you really are a doctor then you know basic triage, Abbey. I have two patients. One has a dislocated knee which may have a fracture running through it, a grazed face, possible injuries I don't know about yet and possible delayed shock. The other has an ulcer that needs dressing. I'm sorry, Abbey. You win. Or you lose. I'm not sure which it is, but either way you're going to hospital.'

They didn't make it.

Abbey submitted to Ryan's plans—after all, she had no choice as she was hardly in a position to hike off to Marg Miller's under her own steam—but halfway down the hill to the hospital a phone rang.

A mobile phone. Ryan started at the sound and looked at where his phone lay on the seat beside him. It wasn't his. Then he looked in the rear-vision mirror and found Abbey removing her phone from her belt.

'Dr Wittner.' Her voice sounded professional and sure.

She really was a doctor, then.

But... Had she said Dr Wittner? Ryan frowned as he listened to her speak. His memory hadn't got her name wrong. Surely she was Abbey Rhodes?

Now wasn't the time for questions. Abbey was snapping out her own questions.

'How bad? Still on the beach? OK, send the ambulance

and tell them to pull out all stops. No, they don't have to collect me on the way. I'm in a car now and we're closer than the ambulance. I'll tell you why later, but the driver'll take me straight there. Ring the surf club back and tell them to keep pouring vinegar—as much as they can and just keep it coming. Prepare ICU and make sure the ambulance has anti-venim and oxygen and adrenalin on board.'

Abbey leaned forward to touch Ryan on the shoulder.

'Ryan, turn around. Now.'

Ryan slowed and stared.

'Why?'

'There's a child been stung by a box jellyfish down on the south beach. He sounds bad.'

'Abbey…' Ryan was rendered almost speechless. 'Abbey, you've just been hit by a car. It's you who's the patient—remember?'

'No.' Abbey's voice was hard and firm. 'Same rules of triage, Ryan. This is urgent. I don't have time to be a patient. I'm the only doctor in this place and unless we get there fast this child could die. Now turn around or let me out and I'll tell the ambulance to pick me up on the way.'

'Abbey…'

'Ryan, surely you remember box jellyfish stings. We'll be lucky if he makes it. Argue later but just *go*.'

The child was on the beach a little way south of the surf lifesaving club. Ryan had spent the three minutes it took to reach there working out just how Abbey would cope. He finally figured she couldn't. And he couldn't either. Box jellyfish stings were right outside his realm.

Box jellyfish—*Chironex fleckeri*—were lethal. Almost invisible in the water, their tentacles stretched up to five metres in length and clung with sticky tenacity to everything they touched. Their venom was lethal. What had Ryan read? You either got enough venom to kill you or you didn't. There was no in between.

Fortunately, the jellyfish were only around in the hottest of the summer months, Ryan remembered, and the popular beaches had stinger nets to keep them at bay. But there were always tourists who preferred to risk swimming outside the nets. That's what must have happened here, Ryan thought. The beach south of the lifesaving club was just as beautiful as the netted area, and when it was deserted it looked much more enticing.

And the current treatment of jellyfish stings? Ryan couldn't think. There wasn't a lot of call for current treatments where he now worked.

Ryan glanced back at Abbey. He was driving fast and the roads were bumpy. The morphine was working but only just. She'd started to regain her colour but was now losing it again.

Ryan's hands whitened on the steering-wheel, saying a silent prayer that her condition wouldn't deteriorate. What if she did have a head injury?

Triage... The box jellyfish victim...

Over the next hill the surf beach lay before them as a wide ribbon of sand, bordered with coconut palms. Ryan saw the group of people clustered on the shore, decided that the worst thing that could happen was that he could bog the car in the sand—and gunned the car right down to where the child lay.

The hire-car people would have a fit if they knew, but Ryan didn't stop until the tyres started spinning in soft sand about three yards from the child.

They'd beaten the ambulance.

Ryan's guess had been right. The child had been swimming in unprotected water. The main beach was two hundred yards further north. This section of beach was deserted, apart from a family group in various stages of hysteria and two lifesavers who must have run from the patrolled beach. They were bent over the child, working hard.

The lifesavers looked up as the car approached, and there was real relief in their eyes.

'Dr Wittner...' One of them breathed Abbey's name as

he saw her, and then paused as he registered that Abbey wasn't driving.

Ryan was out of the car almost before the car stopped, hauling the back door open so that Abbey could see and then stooping quickly over the child.

'Abbey, don't try to get out,' he snapped. 'You can't. Just tell me what to do,' he ordered brusquely, moving as he spoke to check the child's airway and vital signs.

The child—a boy of about thirteen—was unconscious and limp. He'd been wearing a brief costume that only covered his hips. His chest and arms and legs were a mass of angry red weals, and there were traces of tentacle still clinging to his skin.

'Vinegar…' Abbey hauled herself upright on her seat so she could see. Despite Ryan's orders, she'd be out of the car if she could make her damned leg work. She couldn't. 'How much have you used?' she asked the onlookers. Then, as no one answered, she looked down on the sand to where there were two empty flasks and two full ones. She took a deep breath, pushed her faintness aside and raised her voice to command.

'Get all that vinegar on,' she ordered. 'And get the remaining tentacle off.' She was speaking to everyone within hearing distance. 'All of you. Get down on your hands and knees and rub every trace of tentacle off his body. There'll be more venom going in while we watch.'

'You…' She pointed to a gangly boy of about sixteen. 'Pour vinegar over everyone's fingers while they work or you'll be stung yourselves. You…' She pointed to the youngest child—a girl of about twelve. 'Run to the lifesaving club and say you need more vinegar. Scream it. Tell them Dr Wittner says she needs it and she needs it now! There's a shop behind the club. Go up there and yell it, too. Tell them to bring all they've got. Ryan, his breathing…'

'Yeah…' Ryan already knew. The child was half-dead from shock and likely to stop breathing at any minute. 'Is there antivenom?' He was trying to remember. Had there

been antivenom available when he'd lived here as a boy?
He didn't think so.

'Yes,' Abbey snapped, and if her painful leg was causing
her any problem Ryan couldn't hear a trace of it in her
voice. 'It's coming in the ambulance. Just keep him alive
until then. Rod...' Abbey looked across at the senior lifesaver and then winced as a shaft of pain fiercer than the
rest shot up her leg. She shoved away her faintness as ir-
relevant. 'Stand by to do mouth-to-mouth if—'

She didn't have time to say more. The boy stopped
breathing at that moment.

Ryan swore, shot an urgent look up at Rod and moved
to the cardiopulmonary massage position. His hands linked
on the boy's chest and he started thumping down.

'Breathe for him, Rod,' he ordered harshly, hoping
Australian lifesavers still had the training he remembered
undergoing himself as a teenager here.

They did. Rod had a mask at the ready. Standard equipment for a lifesaver at the beach. Now Rod started
breathing—two breaths for every fifteen of Ryan's heart
compresses. Ignoring everything else.

'Move! All of you,' Abbey yelled in a voice that would
have woken the dead. It was a voice designed to do just
that. Ryan's eyes widened as he worked. This was an
Abbey Ryan had never met before—accustomed to emergencies and accustomed to authority. Any doubts as to her
medical training disappeared right then and there.

The family and onlookers were frozen to immobility in
their horror. 'Do what I said,' Abbey ordered harshly.
'Now!'

They moved.

That is, everyone moved except Abbey. She had to stay
on the back seat of the car, watching as everyone else did
her work.

It was driving her crazy, she thought desperately. She'd
never felt so helpless in her life.

Ryan was good, though. Thank God for Ryan...

But, then, if he hadn't been here her leg wouldn't have

been damaged in the first place. At least he was good. There was no way she could fault what he was doing now.

Four minutes… Five… Ryan worked on, hardly pausing for breath, pumping the rhythm on the young boy's heart while Rod breathed steadily through the mask into the boy's mouth.

There was dead silence on the beach.

The child's parents and the other lifesaver were working frantically, rubbing off tiny parts of tentacle from legs and arms and around Ryan's pounding hands, while the older boy kept the affected area awash with vinegar. A small crowd had gathered around, but no one spoke. The parents' faces were streaked with tears, but no one made a sound.

They just worked.

And then there was the sound of the siren. Moments later, the ambulance appeared across the headland and lurched across the beach. It stopped before it reached Ryan's car, the driver clearly worrying more about being bogged down than Ryan had, and in seconds two ambulance officers were running across the sand toward them.

They had what Ryan most needed. Oxygen. Adrenalin. And antivenom.

'Give it to Ryan,' Abbey ordered, pointing at Ryan as the ambulancemen stopped, astounded at the sight of her. 'Dr Henry. He's in charge now.'

And two minutes later the boy started breathing again.

Despite their success, they still couldn't relax. The fact that they had the child breathing again meant little yet in terms of whether he lived or died. The boy was still deeply unconscious but, breathing, he had a chance. That was all they knew. Keeping him breathing gave the antivenim time to work. It meant there was time for a miracle.

He was loaded speedily into the ambulance, and Ryan took charge.

'I'll go with the ambulance,' he said crisply, with only a fleeting thought as to what he should be doing right now. Damn, this was his holiday—his honeymoon, for heaven's sake—but there wasn't a lot of choice here. He looked across at the lifesavers. 'Can one of you bring Dr Rhodes in to the hospital? She has a dislocated knee, possible fracture and possible concussion.' He'd like to take her in the ambulance but if the child stopped breathing again they'd need all the space they had and more.

'Dr Rhodes…?' The ambulance officers looked blank.

'He means me,' Abbey said wearily. 'He's about twenty years out of date. Go on, Ryan.' She motioned to her mobile phone. 'I'll ring the hospital and tell them to expect you. Give you authority to act…'

'Gee, thanks.' It was as wry as he was going to get. Ryan didn't feel wry. He felt railroaded.

Still, this was no time for hesitation. With a last long look at Abbey, Ryan followed the boy's mother into the ambulance. And he gave his last order concerning Abbey. 'Whoever she is,' he growled at the lifesavers, 'take good care of her. And bring her in fast.'

CHAPTER TWO

IT TOOK an hour and a half for Abbey to reach the hospital, and by the time she did Ryan was practically going round the twist.

Not medically.

Sapphire Cove had a beautiful little hospital, with every piece of modern equipment he could hope for. The nursing staff, forewarned by Abbey via mobile phone, greeted him with efficient courtesy, and there was little more Ryan could have done for his jellyfish victim if he'd been back in New York.

Less, he thought grimly. There wasn't a lot of call for jellyfish antivenom on Long Island.

For the first half-hour after he arrived at the hospital his hands were full. The boy took all of his attention. He stopped breathing twice more. Finally, though, the antivenom took effect, his breathing stabilised and a few moments later his eyes flickered open.

His mum burst into tears and, as the boy showed signs of recognising everyone and didn't appear as if he would suffer long-term effects, Ryan felt like doing the same himself. It had been some afternoon.

So where the hell was Abbey?

'She rang in five minutes ago to check everything was OK,' the hospital matron volunteered. A slim, competent woman in her early thirties, Ryan could vaguely remember Eileen McLeod as being a bright spark in his class at school. Only now she was Eileen Roderick.

Like Abbey Rhodes was now Abbey Wittner.

'You told her everything here was OK?'

'Yes. And she's been delayed. Apparently, they had to dig your car out of the sand.' Eileen grinned. 'The tide was coming in and they only just got it free in time. The life-

21

savers wanted to carry Abbey across to another car, but
Abbey wouldn't hear of it and supervised operations from
the back seat.' She grinned again. 'That's our Dr Wittner!
Bossy to the core.'

'So where is she now?' Ryan asked in a voice of fore-
boding. He put his hand up to run long surgeon's fingers
through his thick brown hair. He was tired to the point of
exhaustion. He had to fix Abbey's leg. And he still had to
face his father.

'Rod—the head of the lifesavers—is driving her in, but
she wanted to make a house call first.'

'To Mrs Miller, I'll bet!' Ryan exploded. He crashed one
hand against the door of the nurses' station, making Eileen
jump. 'For Pete's sake—the woman's got a dislocated knee,
if not a broken leg. She's had a thump on the head that'll
give her a headache for a week, if not longer, and she's
haring round the country like there's nothing wrong.'

'She's tough, our Abbey,' Eileen said quietly, and then
cast Ryan a doubtful glance. 'She's had to be.'

Ryan didn't take it up. He didn't care how tough Abbey
was. Twenty-six hours in the air—a car accident—a near-
death—and now...

'She realises I'm waiting to set her leg,' Ryan said
darkly.

'I don't think she realises anything of the kind.' Eileen
looked at him doubtfully. Eileen was the same age as Ryan
and she remembered him from childhood, but she'd always
been a bit in awe of Ryan Henry, even when he'd been
fifteen.

Tall and dark, clever and aloof—that was how Eileen
remembered him. His strong bone structure, dark skin and
good looks, combined with the almost astounding intelligence and sportsmanship he'd displayed at school, had
made him stand apart. It had only been Abbey who'd refused to be intimidated by his solitary air.

Ryan Henry...

Fancy him coming back. Eileen chewed her bottom lip,
trying to think how Ryan's presence could help Abbey.

Eileen and Abbey ran this hospital as a tight-knit team, and maybe only Eileen knew just how hard-pressed Abbey really was.

But local gossip had it that Ryan was here on his honeymoon. That figured. The wonder of it was that Ryan hadn't married years ago. Ryan Henry was tall, dark and rangy. Despite his lean frame, he was strongly muscled and obviously used to the outdoors. His brown eyes crinkled in warm understanding.

His twinkling eyes had even made the boy's unfortunate parents smile a while back, and Eileen had been astounded. Ryan's deep brown hair ran backwards in waves that almost made you want to put your hand up to touch it...

Good grief! Eileen pulled herself up with a start. She was a married lady. What on earth was she thinking of?

'Who does Abbey expect will set her leg, then?' Ryan was saying savagely, and Eileen hauled her thoughts back to Abbey with a visible effort.

'Oh...' Eileen sighed. 'I expect we'll do it together.'

'We?'

'She and me. Or is that—I and her?' Eileen frowned. 'You tell me, Ryan Henry. You were always better at English than me. *Than I.*'

Eileen tossed him her cheeky grin again, and Ryan stared. A nurse who threw back schoolday memories wasn't something he was used to. He expected deference in the hospital where he worked—and he got it.

But Eileen was smiling and he couldn't take offence. Anyway, he had to concentrate. What Eileen was saying didn't make sense.

'Abbey said she stitched her arm herself,' he said blankly, thinking it through.

'She did,' Eileen said. 'Even I was a bit shocked at that one. There was a car smash. Abbey went with the ambulance to the scene and helped get them out. She cut herself badly but didn't let on. There was so much blood no one noticed some of it was hers. She just wrapped it up, didn't say a word and kept on working.

'Afterwards, when we were all exhausted—there were two deaths, you know, and they were locals—Abbey just quietly went away and stitched herself up. It was her right arm, too, and she's right-handed. She didn't do too bad a job either, though it has scarred.'

'Eileen…Sister Roderick.'

'Eileen.' Eileen smiled. 'Heck, Ryan, we go back too far to be formal.'

'Yeah. Eileen.' What was it about calling a nurse by her first name that made him so uncomfortable? 'Eileen, are you saying you approve of Abbey setting her own leg?'

'Well, no. But there's no alternative.'

'She could go to Cairns.'

'An hour and a half's drive?' Eileen shook her head. 'No way. It's crazy if, as you say, the knee is just dislocated. Between us we'll get it back in. What happens here if there's an emergency while she's away? Abbey will refuse point blank to go. Bluntly, Ryan, Abbey hasn't time to waste on herself. She has a baby, there's cows to milk, her mother-in-law needs her—'

'*Stop*!' Ryan put up a hand, as though fending off something he couldn't cope with. 'You're saying Abbey's responsible for all those things?'

'That's right.' Eileen paused and the hospital matron let her smile slip as a thought struck home.

Abbey shrugged her responsibilities off lightly but there was no reason Eileen should do the same for her.

'It's not easy for Abbey, though,' she admitted, looking hopefully up at Ryan. Hey, Ryan was a doctor, after all, and he was planning on being in town for a while. Eileen thought some more, came to sudden urgent conclusions and then she made her voice deliberately doleful. 'And if her leg's as bad as you say it is I have a feeling it'll be impossible.'

'So what will you do while she's laid up?'

'Find her a darned good set of crutches, I guess.' Eileen put her hands on her hips and fixed Ryan Henry with a look. 'Ryan, this place runs because of Abbey Wittner. I don't know if you remember the medical facilities here when you were a kid...'

'I don't remember there being anything here at all,' Ryan confessed, remembering a dreadful car ride to Cairns late at night when his appendix had burst.

'There wasn't anything,' Eileen said bluntly. 'Since Abbey got her medical degree she's organised everything. Galvanised the locals into building this hospital. Restructured the home-nursing service. The medical services in this town are wonderful now—but without Abbey they'll fall apart.'

'But, whether you need her or not, she's just dislocated her knee,' Ryan said faintly. 'Even when we get it back in place she'll have to spend the next week with it up. It'll be so bruised and swollen she won't be able to use it. She'll have to take some time off.'

'She never has before,' Eileen said darkly. 'Not when she had her baby. Not when... Well, not ever. I don't see why she should now. As long as the leg's not broken then I'll help her get it back into place, we'll shove on a Robert Jones bandage to protect it and we'll go on from there.'

'Well, I knocked her off her damned bicycle,' Ryan growled. 'I'll at least have to fix the leg.' Then he met Eileen's suddenly hopeful look and he could read her thoughts as clear as day. 'I am an orthopaedic surgeon, after all,' he said bluntly, 'but that's all I'm doing.'

'Yes, sir,' Eileen said meekly, but she gave him a very long look before she headed back to her work.

An orthopaedic surgeon. Well, well...

Abbey arrived at the hospital half an hour later to find Ryan, pacing. When Rod finally drove Ryan's hire car into the casualty entrance, Ryan grabbed a trolley and almost flung it at the back seat.

'Where the hell have you been?'

There was a note of raw anxiety in his voice but Abbey didn't hear it. All she heard was anger.

'Busy,' she said crisply, hiding the pain in her own voice.

She wasn't letting this man know she'd been silly. She'd thought she could do the house call. But the morphine had worn off and in the end it had been all she could do not to pass out from the pain. 'How's the boy? Eileen says you have him stabilised and the antivenom's working.'

'Yes. Abbey, did you do that damned house call? Are you crazy?' Rod, the head of the lifesavers, had climbed out of the driver's seat and was watching Ryan and Abbey with interest, but Ryan only had eyes for Abbey.

'Mrs Miller wanted to see me,' Abbey said defensively.

'Abbey, she wanted you to dress her ulcer. For heaven's sake…'

'No, she didn't,' Abbey said flatly. 'At least, that wasn't the main reason she wanted to see me. She wanted to tell me something.'

'What?'

'I still don't know,' Abbey confessed. 'Rod was there— well, he had to be—and she clammed up.'

'So you've been wandering round the country—Abbey, you were knocked cold when you came off that bike—and you've been sitting, drinking tea—'

'How did you know I've been drinking tea?'

'Haven't you?'

'Well, yes, but—'

'I guessed,' Ryan said, goaded beyond belief. 'I remember Margaret Miller. Abbey, you are ill and Marg Miller isn't.'

'No, but there's something wrong.'

'But you don't know what?'

'No. But I'll find out.'

'She made me carry her into the kitchen so she could have a cup of tea with the old lady,' Rod said blankly, helping Ryan lift Abbey onto the trolley. 'Doc Wittner propped her leg up on a kitchen chair and went at it like there was nothing wrong. The old lady had the whole thing set up—best china, scones and jam and cream—'

'And I suppose you ate them?' Ryan barked.

'Of course I did.' Abbey glared. 'Marg would have been hurt if I hadn't.'

'And what if I have to give you a general anaesthetic?'

'No one's giving me a general anaesthetic.'

'Says who?'

'Says me.' Abbey glared again. 'Ryan Henry, are you going to take me into the hospital or do I sit here, looking stupid, on this trolley for the rest of the afternoon? I have things to do, even if you don't.'

Ryan ran his hand through his hair.

'Let's push her inside,' Rod said helpfully, 'otherwise she's just as likely to hop off and push the trolley herself. She knows what she wants, our Doc Wittner.'

He gave Ryan a sympathetic man-bossed-by-women grin, and helped the near-speechless Ryan take Abbey into X-Ray.

The bones were intact.

Thanks be, Ryan thought, and Abbey echoed his thought aloud as she stared at the X-ray.

'That's great. I'll have Eileen dose me up with morphine and we'll get it back into position. It'll hardly slow me down at all.'

It was hurting like crazy now but she wasn't admitting to that.

'No way.' Ryan shook his head. '*I'm* putting it back into position. Abbey, I'm an orthopaedic surgeon so lie back, shut up and let me get on with it.'

'An orthopaedic surgeon...' Abbey's face cleared. Despite her bravado, the thought of trying to tell Eileen how to manipulate her leg back into place had had her feeling faint. And she just had to look at Ryan to see he was competent.

She closed her eyes. 'Thank you, Ryan. That'd be great. If you could patch me up before milking...'

Ryan stared. 'Milking...? Abbey, I'll patch you up before bed. That's where you're going and nowhere else.'

'I'm not going to bed.'

'Yes, you are. For a week!'

'That's ridiculous.'

'What's the alternative here, Abbey?' Ryan demanded. 'You produce another bicycle and pedal off into the sunset? You won't even be able to drive.'

'I will.'

'Not while the Robert Jones dressing is on. For a start, the bulk of the thing will hinder you and, bluntly, Abbey, the leg will just be too painful. When we get it back into position you'll be left with residual swelling that'll take a week to go down.'

'I guess.' For a moment Abbey looked worried and then her face cleared. 'Well, I'll just have to cut down on house calls. The ambulance boys can take me out if they need me.'

'Abbey...'

'I'll be fine, Ryan,' she said firmly. 'I have to be.'

'Now that,' Ryan said, in a voice that was just as firm, 'is something I don't understand.' He turned to the matron, who'd just entered the room behind them. 'Eileen, can you prepare me a Robert Jones dressing?' The Robert Jones dressing was a bulky, padded dressing, used to protect the knee and hold it firmly in position.

'Yes, Doctor,' Eileen said primly, casting Abbey a sideways glance, and left Abbey, still arguing.

'Ryan, I am perfectly capable—'

'You're not.' Ryan sat on the edge of the examination couch and caught Abbey's hands. They felt rough. He looked down at her fingers and frowned.

Abbey's hands were work-worn hands. Farmer's hands.

Felicity's hands were silk-smooth, made even more so by expensive moisturisers. Abbey's hands felt like they'd never seen moisturiser in their lives.

Odd how good Abbey's hands felt. How right...

He'd always looked after Abbey.

'I'm fixing this damned leg and cleaning up your face,' Ryan told her gently. 'And then I'm driving you home. And home is where you'll stay. Twenty-four hours' absolute bedrest, Abbey, followed by a week off work with your leg up. Doctor's orders.'

Abbey stared. She looked down at her hands, resting in Ryan's, and something suspiciously like a lump rose in her throat.

Which was stupid. She didn't cry. Not for something as trivial as this.

It must just be the shock of the accident, followed by the drama of the afternoon, she told herself. It certainly wasn't weakness. It certainly wasn't the fact that Ryan might be right.

She closed her eyes and hauled her hands away. When she opened her eyes again she had her facts right.

'I can't,' she said flatly. 'I'm not ill and I don't have a choice here, Ryan. I work.'

'Get a locum,' he said brutally. 'And don't tell me you can't.'

Abbey sighed and shook her head. 'That's just it—I can't. It's November. There'll be no graduating medical students wanting fill-in jobs yet—not until next month when they finish their finals. There are only the professional locum services and they cost an arm and a leg.' She managed a rueful smile. 'And I don't have a leg, Ryan.'

'Well, maybe you can find one who just charges an arm...' Ryan smiled back but shook his head. 'Abbey, that's silly. With this hospital...well, you must be making enough to pay a locum.'

'No.' Abbey's smile faded and her face set. 'And it's none of your business how much I earn. I can't pay a locum and that's that.'

Eileen entered the theatrette again with her hands full of bandages. And her eyes full of mischief.

'What we need is a doctor who'll work for nothing,' she said cheerfully—innocently. 'Maybe someone with local background. Someone with a spot of time on his hands. And someone whose fault it was that our own doctor is out of service...'

Ryan stared.

'Hey, just a minute…' It didn't take Einstein to see what Eileen was on about. 'I'm here on my honeymoon.'

'So we heard, but where's your bride?' Eileen arched her eyebrows. 'Did you leave her sitting by the side of the road when you knocked Abbey off her bike?'

'No. She's still in Hawaii—'

'And she's arriving here later today?'

'No, but—'

'Then what's the problem?' Eileen smiled at Abbey and then smiled at Ryan.

Abbey stared—and Eileen stared right back.

'Don't you dare say we don't need him, Abbey Wittner,' Eileen said firmly, 'because we do. If I can persuade him…' She turned again to Ryan. 'Well, Dr Henry?'

'Eileen, you can't do this,' Abbey said weakly.

'Watch me! Dr Henry will do the right thing. Won't you, Dr Henry?'

Both women looked at Ryan like they expected a rabbit to appear from his hat. And Ryan was left with nowhere to go.

'Hey, if you think you're hijacking my honeymoon,' Ryan expostulated. 'I haven't had a holiday in a year.'

'Dr Wittner hasn't had a holiday for as long as I can remember,' Eileen said solidly. 'And you knocked her off her bike.'

'Eileen, leave him alone,' Abbey said wearily. 'We don't need him.'

'Oh, yes, we do.' Eileen fixed Ryan with her very hardest glare. 'You damaged our doctor, Dr Ryan. Provide us with a replacement model!'

'Eileen!' Abbey was half laughing, half horrified.

But Ryan looked down at Abbey and his protests died. He didn't see her laughter. He saw weariness and pain and need. In fact, he saw absolute exhaustion. Until now he'd thought of himself as tired. This girl was bone-weary.

And she was way too thin. Abbey's eyes were ringed with shadow. Her hands were aged beyond their years with hard physical work.

He saw what Eileen's defiant glare was telling him. And there was no way he could get out of this one.

What on earth would he tell Felicity?

Well, Felicity had already sabotaged the first part of their honeymoon. And now circumstances and these two women were hijacking the rest.

A man knew when he was beaten.

'Very well,' he said wearily. 'I know when I'm licked. Lie back, then, and let me put this damned leg into position, Dr Wittner. From now on it seems you're on my honeymoon!'

Abbey stared up at him. 'What on earth do you mean?'

'I mean I damaged your leg and I'm on holiday,' Ryan said bluntly. 'Or I was on holiday. It seems that now we just swap roles.'

If Ryan had thought Abbey would accept his offer with open arms he was very soon put right. Abbey protested the whole time he and Eileen carefully cleaned, positioned and dressed her leg. In the end, Ryan took drastic measures.

'One more word out of you and we administer a general anaesthetic,' he told her. 'Shut up and keep still.'

Abbey gasped. 'You can't administer a general anaesthetic against my will.'

Ryan sighed and looked across at Eileen. 'Sister Roderick, would you say this patient is behaving unreasonably?'

'I surely would.' Her problems solved, Eileen was now enjoying herself immensely.

'Maybe caused by the bump on her head?'

Eileen nodded. 'Could be.'

'So we—as caring, professional providers of emergency treatment—would be justified in doing whatever we need to administer appropriate treatment.'

Eileen's grin widened. 'Sounds good to me. Short of a sledgehammer, Dr Henry, I'm with you all the way.'

'So shut up, Abbey,' Ryan said kindly. 'You're beaten.' He took the leg carefully between his hands and checked Abbey's face. Abbey had been given a sedative and as much morphine as Ryan thought she could tolerate. He watched her face carefully for signs of pain. None.

With one fast, decisive click, he rotated the lower leg to the right.

Abbey gasped. Her eyes widened in shock—and then she stared down and her pale face creased into a smile. Underneath the swelling the patella looked normal again. One kneecap back in position.

'Well done,' she whispered—and then she went right back to arguing.

'Now let's think this through. If you think I'm lying back and doing nothing—'

'Sister, how far up do you think we should wind this bandage?' Ryan asked. 'How about somewhere near her armpits?'

'Mouth sounds better.' Eileen chuckled.

'Know when you're beaten, Abbey,' Ryan told her, and kept right on winding.

And there was absolutely nothing Abbey could do. So Abbey Wittner finally shut up.

She hardly said a word until Ryan had her in his car, driving northwards towards her home. The jellyfish victim was recovering nicely. Eileen had Ryan's mobile phone number to contact him in an emergency and the transfer of authority was complete. But Abbey didn't like it one bit.

'You don't need to do this,' Abbey told him in a voice that was subdued. In fact, she was tired almost beyond belief. The pain and the shock of the accident was taking its toll, and Ryan's offer to take her home to bed was sounding so good that she wanted to give in to it.

Only she couldn't.

'I do,' Ryan told her. Abbey was stretched out on the back seat of his car again and he was talking to her over his shoulder as he drove. 'Believe me, Abbey, I've looked at it from every angle and I don't see that I can get out of it. You said yourself that the accident was my fault. I was driving too fast.'

'Yeah, but I didn't look—'

'And you now have a massively bruised leg and I have a guilty conscience. So let's fix both, shall we?'

'By letting you be a martyr?' Abbey's voice was sharper than she'd intended and Ryan winced.

That was just how he was feeling—a martyr. Another twinge of guilt hit home.

Should he call what he was doing here martyrdom? This was his home town after all. And he had just squashed the local doctor. Well, Sapphire Cove had been good to him as a child. He owed it something so maybe he could give it, without calling himself a martyr.

'It's not martyrdom, Abbey,' Ryan said, in a voice that was gentler than any he'd used before. 'Let me do it. Please.'

'Be doctor here for a week?'

'Or longer, if you need me.'

'But...you *are* here on your honeymoon,' Abbey said cautiously. 'Everyone knows that. That's why your dad said you were coming.'

'You still know my father?'

'Of course I still know your father.' Abbey cast him a strange look. 'He's a good friend of my mother-in-law. He spends a lot of time with us, and as far as knowing how he is—well, I'd imagine I know him better than you do.'

Ryan's face set. 'Meaning?'

'Meaning he's my friend and he's also my patient.'

Ryan frowned, thinking this through. And accepting, reluctantly, that she was right. She'd have to know his father better than he did. But Abbey as his father's doctor? That took some getting used to.

'Is there anything wrong with him?' he asked.

'Don't you know how his health is?' Abbey demanded. 'He tells me you write to each other'

'Of course we write.'

'Hmm.' Abbey compressed her lips and Ryan could see judgement, standing out a mile. And condemnation. 'So,' she asked, changing the subject, 'where's your bride, then, Dr Henry?'

'In Hawaii.'

'Oh.' Abbey thought this through and then nodded wisely. A doctor-of-the-world nod. 'I see. Separate honeymoons. That's very...very modern.'

'Abbey!'

Abbey hadn't changed one bit, Ryan thought bitterly. Abbey had always said exactly what she'd thought. She'd always told him. And he'd loved her for it.

'Did you get together for the wedding?' Abbey continued, in a voice that was dispassionately interested. Nothing more. 'Or can you do a wedding via teleconferencing these days? Or maybe via the Internet?'

Despite his darkening humour, Ryan couldn't suppress a smile. A teleconferenced wedding! That would be just Felicity's style. Now why hadn't she thought of that?

Abbey's bright eyes were watching him, gently mocking. His smile faded. He went into defence mode. With Abbey, defence had always been a good idea.

'We haven't married yet. We've organised to be married in Sapphire Cove when Felicity gets here.'

'Oh.' To Ryan's surprise, Abbey's face softened. 'Oh, Ryan, your father will like that.'

'I wouldn't imagine he'd care very much.'

'Oh, he'll care,' Abbey said grimly, almost to herself. 'You can't imagine how much.' Then she leaned forward and pointed to a turn-off. 'Here, Ryan. Turn here. This is where I live.'

Ryan stared.

Where Abbey was pointing was to a farmhouse, but it wasn't what you'd call the home of the landed gentry. The farmhouse was a simple cottage, set back among encroaching tropical wilderness. It looked as if it had been built a hundred years ago and nothing much had been done to it since.

There'd been a sugar plantation here once, but not now. Straggling lantana grew wild almost right to the door. There were a few cows in the paddocks around the house. As Ryan turned up the drive poultry scattered in all directions, and a red-headed toddler was pedalling a tricycle along the verandah, scattering hens and feathers in the process.

As the car drew to a halt the toddler stared open-mouthed, bolted inside and reappeared, clutching the hand of someone who had to be his grandma.

The lady he'd produced was in her seventies, still with traces of the child's red hair but bent and weathered with age and Queensland's fierce sun. The woman came down the verandah steps slowly, hobbling with the aid of a walking stick and clutching the small boy to her side in the manner of someone expecting disaster.

This woman had seen disaster, Ryan thought fleetingly as he watched her face. The suffering he saw there was a deeper version of what he saw behind Abbey's eyes. Who was she? He couldn't remember. He couldn't remember anyone living on this place when he was young.

The expression on the woman's face had given way now to open fear. Ryan turned off the engine, but Abbey had the door of the car open before Ryan could move.

'It's OK, Janet,' she called urgently. 'I'm OK. I dislocated my knee but it's fine now.'

Ryan was right. The woman had been expecting trouble. The elderly woman's face cleared, as though she'd just won a reprieve, and she limped the last few steps to the car with a tread that was as close to a bounce as someone who obviously had a damaged hip could manage.

'You've what?'

'I dislocated my knee.' Abbey grinned up at both the woman and the little boy at her side, and only Ryan—who knew how much pain Abbey must still be in—could know what that grin was costing her. 'Hi, Jack. Look what Mummy's done.' Abbey pointed to the bulky bandage which made her leg look three times its size. And then she turned back to the woman. 'Janet, you must remember Ryan Henry. He just knocked me off my bicycle.'

'Ryan Henry...' Janet stared and then her elderly face creased into a smile. 'Of course. Sam's son, Ryan. I remember you as a youngster. You were a bit older than my

John. Welcome home. Though…' She looked doubtfully down at Abbey's leg. 'Did you say Ryan knocked you off your bicycle, Abbey?'

'I did.'

Janet frowned. 'Then I'm not sure whether we should welcome you or tar and feather you and drive you back out of town.'

'There'll be no driving him anywhere,' Abbey said firmly, hauling herself backwards to the edge of the seat. 'Ryan's offered us his honeymoon. Can you give me a hand inside?'

'He's what?' Janet Wittner took a step back. Ryan promptly moved forward and lifted Abbey effortlessly out of the car.

She really was ridiculously slight.

He straightened, holding Abbey in his arms, the hot sun blazing down on them. At their feet the chooks cautiously returned, squawking and fussing in the dust.

'I can't work until this blasted swelling's gone down,' Abbey told Janet from the safety of Ryan's arms. 'Ryan's offered to work for me instead of taking a honeymoon.' She grinned up into Ryan's face and then her smile slipped a little. It felt very strange to be carried against this man's chest. This man whom she'd once known so well. This man whom she'd wept over for months when he'd left her.

'Well, that's very kind of you, Ryan,' Janet told him. 'But won't your wife have something to say about that?'

'He hasn't got a wife yet,' Abbey told her. 'He's left his bride in Hawaii. Ryan, put me down. I can hop.'

'You can't hop anywhere. Except over very flat ground when you can use your crutches, you're to be carried everywhere you need to go for the next few days. Where's your husband?'

Silence.

And Ryan knew that Abbey's husband wasn't in Hawaii. Or anywhere else, for that matter.

Abbey's next words confirmed he'd just put his foot, right in it.

'John's dead,' Abbey said wearily, her brave front suddenly disappearing entirely. 'Thank you, Ryan. If you could just carry me inside then we'll be right now. Thank you for your help.'

CHAPTER THREE

JOHN WITTNER...

Ryan carried Abbey into a house which was as shabby inside as it was out and, as he did, he forced his mind through lists of kids he remembered from his school days. There'd been a few Wittners.

In the end, it was the toddler's red hair that helped. Ryan remembered a boy two years his junior—a big, good-natured youth who'd been great at football and cricket. He'd had brilliant red hair. That was all he remembered of Abbey's husband, but it was enough.

'John Wittner?' he said slowly, as he laid Abbey on her bed. The old lady had stopped out in the living room. Her face had shown her distress as Abbey had said the word 'dead' and she was clearly working at getting her composure back. The toddler, shy of Ryan, had stayed with her. 'Big guy. Six feet three or so. Great at sport.'

'You remember him?' Abbey's eyes showed pleasure as she settled down on the bedcovers. Bed felt just wonderful. And, with luck, she could stay here for half an hour before she needed to start milking.

'Only a little,' Ryan confessed. He sat down on the bed beside her and looked down at his friend. She was so thin! Her short, dark curls were matted with dust and her finely boned face was stretched thin with exhaustion.

But her clear blue eyes looked up at him and she was still the same Abbey.

Abbey... Seventeen years of absence and she was still his friend. It distressed him unutterably to know she'd been in trouble and he hadn't known. Abbey lay there, dirty, bruised and way too thin, and he remembered just how he'd felt about her all those years ago.

He'd loved her.

'Tell me about John,' he said quietly. 'When were you married?'

'After I graduated.' Abbey shrugged. 'John...well, John had the biggest heart. After you left...' She caught herself remembering how she'd felt when Ryan had left, and she couldn't stop the pain washing over her face. Let Ryan think it was just her leg...

'Well, I needed a friend,' she managed. 'And John...well, he sort of became it. Then my mum died...'

'Your mother died?'

'She died of cancer when I was twelve. And the Wittners took me in. Janet treated me like her own, and John and I...well, we just drifted from friendship into marriage. It was like it was meant. Only...'

'Only?'

Abbey took a deep breath and closed her eyes. 'While I was away at medical school John's dad died. Janet didn't cope very well. She'd depended heavily on John's dad and she lost interest in everything. John kept on farming but suddenly every decision was his. The transition was too sudden.'

'He got into financial trouble?' Ryan's voice was intent. He was watching the pain wash over Abbey's face, and part of him didn't want to hear the end of the story.

'The Wittners had a lovely farm. They grew sugar cane and ran cattle,' Abbey said bleakly, as if telling a story that still had the power to hurt. 'The farm was prosperous, but John didn't have much of a head for figures. He made a few investments that weren't very wise and he gave loans to people he shouldn't have trusted. By the time I finished medical school and came back here to marry him he was in real trouble.'

'So you sold up and moved here.'

'It wasn't quite as simple as that,' Abbey confessed. 'John... Well, he was proud and he wouldn't let on to either Janet or me just how much trouble he was in. I galvanised the community into building the hospital, my medical practice started paying and then I found myself pregnant. I was delighted and I thought John was, too. With the farm and my medicine, there seemed to be heaps of money. But…' Her voice faltered and Ryan found himself covering her hand on the bedclothes.

'Tell me, Abbey.'

'When John ran into trouble he started gambling,' Abbey said painfully. 'No one knew. He just… I was busy and he'd go away—to farming conferences, he said, and we believed him. And then he ran so deeply into debt it was a nightmare and he still couldn't tell us.' Her voice faltered. 'And then he shot himself.'

'Oh, Abbey…'

'He didn't even make a good job of that,' Abbey said wearily. 'He was in a coma for months before he died. The place was a financial disaster, there wasn't any insurance and I was pregnant. Jack was born two months after John died.' She shrugged, putting aside a nightmare.

'So the bank foreclosed and Janet and I sold up. Janet couldn't bear to live in town. She thinks everyone is still talking about her and she can't bear to face people or talk about John. The only person she'll still see is your father.'

'So…we bought this place, which was all we could afford—and here we are. Apart from a pile of debts which I'm slowly paying off, then we're fine. We're doing fine.' She spread her hands. 'I'm sorry. It's the end of a rotten story.'

Only it wasn't. Ryan looked down at those work-weary hands and knew that it wasn't.

'Are you making ends meet now?' he asked gently, and Abbey grimaced.

'We will. Apart from my medical income, we're supplying a local cheesemaker with unpasteurised milk and…'

'How many cows are you milking?'

'Fifteen. That's all the milk he wants and it's not enough for one of the bigger dairies to adjust their collection procedures.'

'Fifteen cows?' Ryan frowned, thinking this through. 'But that's hardly enough to justify milking machines.'

'Well, isn't that lucky?' Abbey managed a smile. 'We milk by hand.'

'You have to be kidding!'

'No.' Abbey sighed again. 'Look, if we get rid of the farm entirely I think Janet will just curl up and die. She loves Jack and she loves the farm.'

'Abbey, Janet's hands…her hip…'

'Yes?' Abbey's voice was disinterested and weary. Twenty more minutes until she had to face the cows…

'Abbey, Janet's hands are crippled with arthritis. Her hip seems even worse than her hands.'

'So?'

'She can't possibly milk.'

'No. I do that.'

'That's ridiculous,' Ryan exploded. 'You can't milk twice a day and run a medical practice and care for a—'

'What's the choice here, Ryan?'

Silence.

'There has to be a choice,' Ryan said at last. He thought of Felicity—of what she'd say, presented with this nightmare. It didn't bear thinking of. 'You'll have to buy a small house in town…'

'I told you—we can't live in town. Janet can't bear it. And this place was cheaper than anything within the town boundaries.' Abbey cast a rueful glance around at the rising damp on the walls and the cracks in the plaster. 'Much cheaper. This way—well, the cows bring in an income. Janet thinks she's making a contribution—as indeed she is. She cares for the poultry and sells the eggs and she cares for Jack when I'm away…'

'And you do all your house calls by bicycle!'

'I have a car,' Abbey said defensively. 'I just don't use it when I can use the bike.'

'You can't tell me you wouldn't make more and have an easier life living in an apartment in town.'

'*I* might,' Abbey said evenly. 'Jack and I could live in a flat at the back of the hospital. But where would that leave Janet?'

'She's old enough for a nursing home.' That's what Felicity would do, Ryan knew. Get the hell out of the mess. Abandon the old lady and leave the whole catastrophe behind her so fast you wouldn't see her for dust.

Silence again.

Then Abbey shook her head, nestled her head back down on the pillows. And closed her eyes.

'Go away, Ryan Henry,' she said wearily. 'I'd appreciate it if you would care for the medical needs of the town for the next week. I'd appreciate it very much. But that doesn't mean I have to spend any time with you.'

'Why the hell—?'

'Ryan, for a minute there then you sounded just like your mother,' Abbey told him flatly. 'And if there's one person in this world I could never stand it's your mother.'

Ryan rose, anger flooding into his face. 'If it comes to that—'

'Yeah, my mother was a slut,' Abbey said in the same disinterested tone. 'Your mother told me she was so you don't need to repeat it. Go away, Ryan.'

'Abbey…'

'Oh, leave it.' Abbey was bone-tired and she wanted done with it. The sight of this man beside her bed was doing strange things to her insides. She wanted to weep. Her leg throbbed and the world just seemed too darned hard.

'Who's milking tonight?' Ryan's face had closed and his tone was clipped. There was anger in his voice but also resignation. He wasn't enjoying this one bit—but, damn, he'd do the right thing by this girl. And then he'd leave.

'Who do you think?' Abbey demanded dully. 'Me? Me? Or maybe you think it's me. Now go away so I can have fifteen minutes to pull myself together before I have to start.'

'You can't milk tonight.'

'Well, that leaves Janet and Jack to do it for me. You choose!'

'There must be someone else…'

'There isn't. Go away.' And Abbey humped herself over and faced the wall. Good grief, she thought bleakly. She was behaving like a petulant child—but that was how Ryan made her feel. Like her life was way out of control, and her problems were exposed for all the world to see. For Ryan to see.

She didn't like this.

Abbey blinked back a stupid tear. And then another.

'Can Janet show me what to do?' Ryan asked, and his voice sounded like it came from a long way off.

Abbey sniffed and tried to focus on what he'd said.

'What do you mean?'

'I assume Janet can give me directions on how to get your cows in, and I vaguely remember milking the house cow as a boy. It's like riding a bicycle, isn't it? Once learned, never forgotten.'

Ryan wasn't a long way away at all. His hand came down and touched Abbey's cheek, wiping tears from her long lashes. There was resignation in his voice, but also tenderness. 'Abbey, go to sleep. I'll go and milk your damned cows for you. And then…after that we'll sit down and try to make some sense out of this mess!'

'You don't… You can't…' Abbey twisted around on the bed but Ryan's hands held her firm.

'Abbey, shut up and go to sleep,' he said kindly. 'I'm the senior doctor here—remember? What I say goes. Now just cut out the protests and go to sleep.'

It was all Abbey wanted to do. It was all her body was screaming at her to do.

She looked up into Ryan's concerned face and for the life of her she couldn't think of a thing to say. Or do. The morphine was blurring her edges. Muting her protests. She blinked and tried, but all that would come out was what she most wanted to say.

'Yes, sir,' she said. 'Thank you.'

And the morphine took its toll. She slept.

Abbey woke to laughter.

She stirred and winced and checked herself out from the toes up.

Her leg was hurting. So was her face. Nothing too drastic, though. The dressing Ryan had put on her face was stretched—the swelling must have pulled the cover tight. She winced and adjusted it, loosening it and reapplying the sticky edges. Then she tried moving her leg.

It didn't hurt as much as she'd expected. The huge dressing was holding everything firm.

She was covered by a thick quilt. It hadn't been there when she'd gone to sleep. Janet must have come in...

Or Ryan had put it over her.

Abbey found herself flushing at the thought of Ryan, being beside her when she was asleep. No. It had to be Janet.

Ryan Henry...

He'd slammed back into her life with the force of a bulldozer and it wasn't the knock on her head this afternoon that was making her dizzy. Ryan....

'Don't be stupid, Abbey Wittner,' she told herself harshly. 'Just because the man's good-looking and smiles just the way he used to... It doesn't mean he's the same. It doesn't mean you still have to be in love with him...'

There were giggles coming from the kitchen. Abbey listened for a whole two minutes and then could bear it no longer. She grabbed the hospital crutches from the bedside and staggered forth, her first venture on four legs.

Ryan Henry was seated at Abbey's kitchen table and he was feeding her son.

Abbey stopped at the kitchen door and blinked, and blinked again. Janet was smiling with pleasure while Ryan aeroplaned Jack's egg into his mouth. It was hard to know who was having the most fun—Jack, Jack's grandma, Janet or the man with the egg aeroplanes.

'Jack doesn't like egg,' Abbey said slowly, and Ryan and Janet turned towards her. Not Jack. Her little son didn't look up. The toddler was concentrating fiercely on catching and eating the next aeroplane.

Jack doesn't like egg?

'More,' said Jack.

'Says who?' Ryan asked politely. He gave Abbey a mocking smile and went back to his aeronautics. Jack demolished the last mouthful of egg and crowed with delight.

'Ryan does a finer aeroplane than you or I ever did.' Janet's smile deepened as she stood and shifted awkwardly to the stove. 'Sit down, child, and I'll give you your dinner. I kept it hot.'

Abbey frowned and looked at the clock above the big old fire stove. And winced.

Seven o'clock!

'We let you sleep,' Janet explained. 'We thought it was best.'

'I see.' Abbey didn't see at all. She looked at Ryan with suspicion. 'Did Janet feed you, then?'

'There's no need to say it like it's taking food from your mouths,' Ryan complained. 'Janet said there was heaps.'

'And so there is,' Janet said warmly. 'Ryan's milked all the cows and it's only taken him two and a half hours to do it.'

'Two and a half...' Abbey's eyes widened and twinkled. 'Did the girls give you a hard time, Ryan?'

'They learned who was boss,' Ryan said evenly. 'Eventually.'

'He might need a loan of your crutches or my walking stick,' Janet interjected. 'He got himself kicked.'

Abbey lifted her brows in sympathetic enquiry. 'Really? Badly, Ryan? Let me see.'

'No way,' Ryan said darkly. 'And don't ask where. Enough to say it's a place where the sun rarely shines. It's not crutches I need but a gynaecological pillow.'

A gynaecological pillow was a pillow shaped like an inner tyre to take the pressure from sore bottoms after childbirth. Abbey grinned in swift sympathy.

'Oh, dear.'

'He was bending over to tie one girl's legs and he forgot the girl in the next bail wasn't tied,' Janet explained. She looked over at Abbey and her eyes twinkled. She chuckled out loud and Abbey's eyes widened even further. It had been a long time since she'd heard Janet chuckle.

Janet placed a plate of casserole on the table. Abbey lowered herself thoughtfully into the chair and surveyed her family.

It all seemed so…so domestic. To have Ryan sitting in the chair at the other end of the table, calmly wiping superfluous egg from her son's little face. The kitchen had been empty…well, it had *seemed* empty since they'd moved here. Ryan filled John's place and more, his charismatic presence holding Janet and the baby spellbound.

And what about Abbey herself?

She had loved this man once, she conceded. Or maybe that was wrong. She'd loved this *boy* before he'd become a man. This boy was now a surgeon—a career-oriented doctor, engaged to be married to a woman in Hawaii and home for only two weeks.

Home?

No. This wasn't Ryan's home. This was his honeymoon destination. Abbey gave herself a fast mental shake. It was no use growing accustomed to Ryan being at her kitchen table. In two weeks he'd be gone.

Once, many years ago, she'd broken her heart over his leaving. Not any more. Now she didn't even know him.

'Your leg's hurting,' Ryan said softly, and Abbey flushed as she realised he'd been watching her.

'N-no.' she lied. 'Well, maybe just a bit.'

'Do you want more morphine?'

'No.' She shook her head. 'I'll take aspirin if I need to.'

'Aspirin's not strong enough, Abbey.' Once again, that cool voice which held a hint of concern—a voice that was close to Abbey's undoing. The same voice she remembered from all those years ago. 'It's no weakness to admit you're in pain. And there'll be scratches and bruises under that filthy T-shirt. Would you like me to help you bath?'

'No way!' She blinked, determined. 'And I'll stick to

aspirin, thanks very much. Morphine will just make me go
to sleep.'

'That's just what you need to do, girl,' Janet said
strongly, and Abbey shook her head.

'No. I have to bath Jack and put him—'

'In case you haven't noticed, Jack's in his pyjamas,'
Janet told her. 'Ryan and I have already bathed Jack.'

Abbey blinked. 'You!' Her eyes swivelled to Ryan.

'There's no need to sound as if you think I'm completely
useless,' Ryan complained. 'I can cope with the odd baby
bath.'

'Yeah?' Abbey gave him a sideways look. 'How many
babies have you bathed in your time, Ryan Henry?'

'One,' he said promptly. 'But it was a brilliant one,
wasn't it, Jack?' He grinned down at Abbey's little son and
Jack grinned a toothy toddler smile right back at him.

'I...I see.' Abbey couldn't help staring. This man was
making himself right at home. Jack was normally shy...

'It wasn't all that brilliant,' Janet conceded. 'I told him
what to do.'

'Not necessary.'

'It was necessary, young Ryan,' Janet told him, and Ryan
smiled and sat back in his chair like a rebuked schoolboy.
'I just wish I could do it myself.' Janet's smile faded. 'If I
could lift him...'

'He's too heavy for you to lift from the bath,' Abbey
said, as if repeating a conversation that had been played
out a hundred times. 'But, Janet, if you'd get your hip
fixed...'

'Your hip?' Ryan turned to look consideringly at Janet.
'Now that's what I don't understand. Tell me why you're
dependent on sticks.'

'Arthritis,' Janet said shortly. 'It doesn't matter.'

'It does.' Abbey leaned forward and spoke urgently to
Ryan. 'Janet's in urgent need of a hip replacement. If she
had that...well, she'd be like a girl again. But I can't persuade her to get it done.'

'I'd have to go to Cairns,' Janet said harshly, 'and I won't leave you, girl. You need me.'

'I can get a babysitter...'

'For a month or more? And who'd feed the poultry and look after Jack and—?'

'Who'll push your wheelchair when your leg gives completely?' Abbey retorted.

Ryan held up a hand. 'Whoa... Is there something I'm missing here?'

'Yes,' Abbey said shortly. 'Or rather—no. There are no complications. She should get it done and she won't.'

'I won't go to Cairns,' Janet muttered. 'I'd hate it.'

'I'd come and visit you,' Abbey told her.

'Oh, yes,' Janet jeered. 'In your spare time?'

'Why not do it here?' Ryan asked, and both women turned to stare at him.

Silence.

It was Abbey who spoke first.

'Well, that's a crazy suggestion,' she said simply. 'Firstly, I'm the only doctor here and I can't operate and give anaesthetic at the same time. Secondly, and more importantly, I'm not a surgeon, much less an orthopaedic surgeon with the skills to do hip replacements. I can do an appendicectomy in an absolute emergency, with my charge sister giving anaesthetic, but that's an end to it. With my knowledge of orthopaedics, I'd end up having Janet walking backwards.'

Ryan smiled, but his smile was perfunctory. 'I could, though,' he said. 'I told you when I put your knee back, Abbey. My specialty's orthopaedics.'

More silence.

'Oh, yes?' Abbey said finally, and her voice was faintly mocking. This was cruel. 'Maybe you could. *If* we had the equipment. *If* we had an anaesthetist and back-up staff. *If* you were registered to work here. *If* pigs flew!'

'Registered...' Ryan centred on only one objection. 'If I can organise everything else, is registration likely to be a problem?'

'Well, maybe not,' Abbey admitted. 'You're not Australian trained, but with your Australian citizenship, your training and the fact that we're a remote hospital…'

'Remote?'

'It's why I accepted your offer of help this week,' Abbey explained. 'Because Sapphire Cove's categorised as remote, if any doctor is stupid en— I mean, willing enough to work here and their basic overseas training is acceptable, we can get their registration through in a flash.'

'I see.' Ryan's magnetic grin flashed out. 'So…I've just offered to be stupid.'

'I'm not having any hip operated on,' Janet broke in harshly. She'd been staring from Abbey to Ryan in confusion. 'Abbey, this is crazy. Who'd look after Jack if I was in hospital?'

'If Ryan can organise a few pigs to fly I don't see why you should object,' Abbey said promptly. '*If*! But Ryan's doing my work for me. Didn't you hear him offer? And Marcia over the road was put off work last week. The resorts always lay off staff during stinger season. Janet, let's not throw any more obstacles in his way than Ryan already has. He's offered me his honeymoon and you a new hip. What next?'

What next, indeed?

Ryan sat at the table as Janet and Abbey talked across him, and he felt as if he'd been knocked sideways.

Why on earth had he made that offer?

To do a hip replacement here…in such a place…

It wasn't that he doubted his ability to organise it. Routine procedures such as hip replacements were now left to those working under him and there were favours he could call in to get equipment and staff. It was just…

Well, this was his honeymoon, after all. He'd have to beg, borrow or steal equipment from a bigger hospital. Pull in favours from all over the place. It'd take a couple of days to get everything he needed. At a guess, Felicity would arrive just as he'd lined up Theatre.

Felicity would not be happy.

But Abbey was.

Ryan looked over the table and Abbey's eyes were misting as she looked at her mother-in-law. And then Abbey turned to look at him.

'If you could organise it, it'd be the best thing...' she said, and her voice shook.

Ryan's astonishment at what he'd just offered lifted a little.

He'd eased just a fraction of the load on Abbey's slight shoulders and for some reason—well, for some reason he suddenly didn't give a toss what Felicity would say. He had to do it. He felt lighter himself.

And then the phone rang.

One thing Ryan had learned early in medical school was that the most emotional moments of his life—or the most embarrassing—were always punctuated with the phone.

The mobile phone shrilled, and both Abbey and Ryan looked down at their waists.

Abbey grinned and held up her hands.

'You win,' she said, as Ryan flipped his phone open.

Then her smile faded as she watched Ryan's face.

'Ryan, what is it?'

Ryan was talking harshly into the phone.

'They're already bringing him in? OK, I'll be there as fast as I can.'

And Ryan was on his feet, his chair clattering to the floor behind him. He didn't even notice that he'd knocked it over.

'What is it?' It had to be something awful, Abbey knew. All the colour had drained out of Ryan's face.

'It's my father,' he said shortly. 'It sounds like he's had a heart attack.'

'Oh, no...' Janet went white and automatically clutched Jack, as if clutching the baby could ward off catastrophe.

'Not another one.' Abbey rose too, grabbing her crutches and shoving them under her arms. 'Ryan, give me a hand out to the car.'

Ryan stopped dead, and stared back at Abbey. His face

had grown suddenly haggard. 'What do you mean—another?'

'He's had three this year,' Abbey told him bluntly. 'He's running on borrowed time.'

'But—'

'Ryan, shut up and move,' Abbey ordered. She gave Jack a fast pat goodbye. 'See you later, sweetheart. Mummy has to go back to the hospital. Be good for Gran. Janet, I'll look after Sam for you, I swear. Don't worry.' And Abbey grabbed her crutches and headed for the door.

'You're not coming,' Ryan said automatically, but Abbey was already on her way.

'Just help me into the damned car,' she said harshly. 'I'm not leaving you to look after your own father and, besides, Janet and I love Sam Henry.'

And what Abbey didn't say—and both of them knew— was that if Sam was in real trouble then Ryan could become next to useless. To be an efficient doctor was an impossibility when the patient was so close.

And if hard decisions had to be made...if life support systems had to be shut down...

Well, Abbey was coming!

Ryan was so shocked he didn't speak again until they were halfway to the hospital.

When he did he sounded sick.

'Tell me Dad's medical history, Abbey.'

With Ryan's help, Abbey had hauled herself into the back seat again, her leg stretched out before her. Her position hadn't been achieved without cost. From the hip down, her leg was starting to ache as it had before the morphine, a dull, rhythmic throb.

'Don't you know?' She shifted and winced.

'I didn't even know he had a heart problem.' Ryan swore savagely. 'So tell me!'

Ryan didn't know? Abbey shook her head in concern. How much didn't he know?

'Well, Sam's like Janet,' Abbey said slowly, 'only it's

more drastic. He desperately needs by-pass surgery but he won't have it.'

'Why not?'

Abbey shrugged. 'He says it's because he doesn't want to leave the farm. Myself, I think it's more than that.'

'What do you mean?'

'I mean he's a lonely old man with no family,' Abbey said gently. 'He's fond of Janet and Jack and me, but we're all he has and we're not enough. I don't think he wants to live to a ripe old age.'

'But that's...' Ryan shook his head. 'That's...'

'Nonsense?' Abbey shrugged. 'Well, I guess you'd know better than I do. You're his son, after all. But, then, you're his son and you didn't even know he had a heart condition.'

'I write,' Ryan said explosively. 'I write every week.'

Abbey screwed up her nose. She knew about those letters. 'Yes, you do,' she said gently. 'I'm sure your concern does you credit.'

'Abbey...'

'Why has he had a heart attack now?' Abbey asked, staring into the middle distance over Ryan's shoulder. 'Has he been stressed?'

'How the hell should I know?'

'There you are, then.'

'Damn it, Abbey...'

Abbey ignored his mounting anger. Someone had to lay the truth before Ryan Henry. A letter once a week... Sam had shown her a few. Proudly. And Abbey had felt sick inside when she'd seen them.

They were formal, punctilious letters, describing Ryan's career, the weather, the news wherever Ryan happened to be in the world. Always a polite enquiry after his father's health at the end.

They were duty letters. The fact that Sam had been proud of them had made Abbey cringe inside.

'How was he today, though?' Abbey probed. 'Was he happy to see you? Relaxed?'

'I haven't seen him yet,' Ryan said explosively. 'I hit a bicyclist on the way into town—remember?'

'Oh, yes.' But Abbey didn't sound apologetic in the least. She kept right on probing. 'So—did he mind when you let him know you'd be late?'

'I didn't let him know...'

Silence.

'You mean...' Abbey's voice grew softer. 'Ryan, Sam told me he was expecting you about midday. He's been talking of nothing else for weeks. He's been talking of his son coming home. Waiting. And what time is it now? Eight? He'll have been pacing the floor—'

'I was milking your cows, dammit.'

Abbey bit back her anger with real difficulty. 'I know and I'm grateful but... Ryan, how long would it have taken you to phone him—to tell him you'd be eight hours late? How long, Ryan Henry? You didn't even think.'

'I had to milk your cows. And you didn't tell me—'

'I didn't tell you that your father has a bad heart and you should ring and reassure him?' Abbey took a deep breath. Her leg was on fire and her anger was building to boiling point. She'd watched Sam Henry pine for his family for almost twenty years and she hadn't been able to do a damned thing about it. And now Ryan was sitting in the driving seat, practically saying it was her fault Sam had this attack.

She wasn't going to yell. She wouldn't!

'How could I have said that to you without sounding like a patronising adult talking to an uncaring, unthinking child?' she asked finally, and her voice was deathly quiet. 'I wish I'd known that's exactly what you are!'

And after that there was nothing—absolutely nothing—left to say.

CHAPTER FOUR

SAM HENRY was in Intensive Care when they arrived. His worry and anger building to a crescendo, Ryan abandoned Abbey in the car and strode down the hospital corridor fast, the night charge sister by his side.

Ryan looked every inch a doctor, Abbey thought as she watched him go, walking as all hospital staff were taught to move in an emergency. Walk fast—never run. Never risk barrelling into patients and making things worse.

There was more than the way he moved that showed the world Ryan was a doctor, though. Ryan Henry exuded authority and competence. The night sister automatically deferred to him when they arrived, without once looking at Abbey for confirmation of his authority.

All Ryan needed was a white coat and stethoscope hanging around his neck and he might have been the doctor in charge here for years.

He was all doctor, and Abbey hardly knew him. This man she had once known almost as well as she'd known herself...

Once, long ago, Abbey had loved Ryan Henry, she thought sadly as she watched him disappear around a turn in the corridor. The boy Abbey knew had loved his father absolutely and would never hurt him.

Where was the boy Abbey had loved now? Had he disappeared for ever?

It didn't matter. It couldn't matter. The old Ryan was part of her childhood. Nothing more.

Abbey had been abandoned in the car in the casualty entrance and now there was nothing to do but wait. Her leg hurt too much to move unless she had to. She knew if Ryan needed her he'd remember her presence and send someone out to fetch her.

In the end, he didn't need to. The ward attendant came out to move Ryan's car—and stopped in astonishment when he saw her.

'Doc Wittner!'

'Yeah,' Abbey gave him a reluctant grin. 'Hi, Ted. Do you think you could help me inside?'

'Sure.' Ted stared down at her, his face creasing in concern. 'But... I didn't think you were supposed to be here. Aren't you supposed to be home in bed? Eileen said you'd been injured.'

'Just a bruised knee. And I want to know what's going on inside.'

'Doc Henry's looking after his father.'

'Sam's OK?'

'I dunno,' Ted admitted. 'All I know is they haven't called me to shift him to a slab yet so that's gotta be a good sign.'

Abbey grinned. Ted was a wizened Korean War veteran who'd been a semi-invalid ever since. Lonely and miserable all his life, when Abbey had offered him the job as ward attendant he'd been astounded. 'Who, me? I couldn't do anything like that in a pink fit.' It had taken all Abbey's skills at persuasion to have him give the job a go.

Since then Ted had been Abbey's most loyal employee. He lived in a tiny apartment at the back of the hospital and the hospital was now his world. But there were no greys in Ted's world. There was black and white. Dead or alive.

Sam was alive.

'You want a trolley?' Ted asked her dubiously, eyeing her huge white leg, and Abbey shook her head.

'No, but a wheelchair would be good. And a hand backwards out of this car.'

'No sooner said than done.' A minute later Abbey's wheelchair was spinning down the corridor to Intensive Care.

Sam was definitely still alive.

Ted pushed the ward door open and Abbey looked in with some trepidation, to find Sam Henry looking to see who'd just entered. When Sam saw Abbey his face puckered into a white-faced smile.

'Hey, Abbey...'

'Sam.' Abbey shoved the wheels of her chair down to push herself over to the bed. She took Sam's hand in hers. It was clammy and cold but he was alive, and for the moment that was all that mattered.

In the last few years Abbey had leaned heavily on Sam Henry for advice and friendship. In fact, Sam had become almost as important to Abbey as his son had once been.

'What on earth are you doing to us now?' she asked gently.

'Damned heart,' Sam whispered, 'but Ryan's here.' The old man looked up at Ryan, standing beside his bed, and there was no mistaking the pride and love in his voice.

Abbey looked up too, and saw Ryan's face set. Ryan had heard it, then. The love and the pride. The ties that went far beyond duty letters. And Abbey saw in his face that Ryan was feeling just dreadful.

The old Ryan wasn't completely gone.

OK. She'd let Ryan off the hook. Take the blame herself. Let Sam keep on thinking that his son was wonderful.

'I'm so sorry.' Abbey squeezed Sam's hand. 'Did Ryan tell you it was all my fault he was late? First I smashed my bike into him. Then I demanded he put my dislocated knee back into place, and finally he had to milk my cows. And all the time you were waiting and not knowing he was even in the district. I'm so sorry.'

'There's no damage.' There *was* damage, Abbey knew. Sam's voice was a weak whisper, but there was no way he'd conceded anything to his dicky heart in the past. He wasn't about to start now. 'I might have known Ryan was needed. He wouldn't have been late otherwise. My Ryan's a great boy.'

'He is, too.' Abbey ventured a smile up at Ryan and found his face still looked as if it were carved in stone. Pain was washing over her in waves. Soundlessly Ryan held out the ECG reading. Abbey checked it carefully, and nodded.

'It's OK, Ryan,' she told him. 'Not much different to last time.' A little worse. Not much.

'What the hell...?' Ryan's voice was full of pent-up emotion. 'Dad...you've got a heart that's as dicky as this and you haven't even told me?'

'Now hardly seems the time to yell at him for being a bad letter-writer,' Abbey said mildly. She smiled affectionately at Sam. 'I'll yell at you in the morning, if you like. For now I'll ring Janet and let her know you're OK. She'll be worried so I'll thank you kindly to stop scaring her. If Ryan's done all he needs maybe you should get some sleep.'

'I don't need all these wires,' Sam said fretfully, and Abbey fixed him with a look.

'Yes, you do.'

'Why?'

'Because they keep your son happy,' Abbey told him. 'Also they tell us that your heart's still beating, and if Ted out there doesn't have positive proof of a beating heart every few minutes or so he has a nice little slab down in the mortuary that's just your size.'

Silence. Ryan's eyebrows hit his hairline.

But, to her satisfaction, Sam gave a weak chuckle. 'You always did have such a persuasive way with you, young Abbey,' he whispered. 'OK, then. I'll wear your dratted wires. Now get off with you and let a man get to sleep.'

'Do you always gain patient compliance by threatening them with the mortuary?' Ryan asked as he wheeled Abbey back into the corridor. His voice sounded drained and weary, but also calmer. The electrodes attached to Sam's chest were giving a cautiously optimistic message. A nurse was sitting beside Sam's bed and there was every reason to hope he'd live a bit longer. Live to be persuaded to have his by-pass...

'I use it all the time.' Abbey chuckled. 'Works a treat.

Especially since Ted started taking guided tours of his underground room.'

'Ted...' Ryan frowned. 'Is that the ghoul I saw, stalking the hospital corridors, as I came in?'

'If he looked like a ghoul it was definitely Ted.'

Ryan frowned. 'He looks familiar. Do I...did I know him?'

'Probably,' Abbey told him, 'but I wouldn't imagine you were on close terms. He's Ted Hammond.'

The wheelchair came to an abrupt halt. Ryan stared down in incredulity. 'Abbey, Ted Hammond was a derelict when I was a kid. How—?'

'He wasn't a derelict,' Abbey said. 'He was just bored and lonely. He was out of work and didn't know how to fill in his time. Ted came back from the war to find his wife and kids had left him. He had one leg shorter than the other and he had nerve damage. So...he drifted on the streets and he stayed there. Then...'

'Yeah, tell me what happened then.' Ryan straightened and started walking again—and Abbey frowned. It was a strange sensation, being wheeled by Ryan Henry.

Concentrate on Ted...

'Well, a couple of months after the hospital opened we had an awful car crash down near the beach,' Abbey told him. 'Ted was first on the scene. When I got there with the ambulance Ted had hauled a couple of kids clear before the car burst into flames. There were a couple of others dead inside. Ted coped—in fact, he coped a lot better than I or the ambulance officers did. And I saw a side that he'd kept hidden for years behind a wall of misery. So I offered him a job.'

'Abbey, he was a street bum...'

'No. He was a lonely old man without friends and family and without an aim,' Abbey said roundly. 'People like your mother classified him as a bum while he was ill and desperate, and the label just stuck. Ted didn't drink. He just didn't know what else to do with himself but sit on park benches and look desolate. And if he looked unkempt it was because he couldn't see the point of being anything else. He's not unkempt now.'

Silence.

Oh, dear. Abbey bit her lip. She'd just criticised Ryan's mother—again. She and Ryan were doomed not to be friends any more, Abbey thought miserably. Then she looked up as the night sister approached.

'Sister?'

'I was just wondering,' the nurse said, and smiled shyly up at Ryan. 'Dr Henry, are you going home?'

'I thought I'd check our jellyfish victim once more, then take Dr Wittner home and go on to sleep at my father's,' Ryan said brusquely, still mulling over Abbey's words. He motioned to the phone on his belt. 'Call me if you need me.'

The nurse hesitated. 'But…'

'Ryan, when I have someone in hospital with heart problems I don't go home,' Abbey interjected. 'And the jellyfish toxin is still a risk, despite the antivenom. So, as you're now doctor in lieu of me…'

'Abbey…'

'Ryan, I don't know whether you realise what you've let yourself in for here,' Abbey told him. 'You're *it*. There's no resident or intern backing you up. If your father goes into cardiac arrest then there's only you.'

Ryan frowned. Sleep at the hospital? He'd never thought of doing that.

But if he didn't? If his father went into cardiac arrest? Trained nurses could start emergency procedures but…

Abbey was right. To drive the five minutes to take Abbey home was one thing. To be fifteen minutes out of range at his father's house…

He hardly had a choice here. But if he had to stay at the hospital for the entire week…well, Felicity would not be pleased.

'What do you do with your little boy when you need to stay here?' he asked, and Abbey shrugged.

'If I can, I bring Jack with me and settle him into the

children's ward. That's possible if I have warning but Janet copes if there's not time to bring him. She can't bath him, but she can do most other things. He helps her by climbing in and out of his own cot now.'

'But you milk.'

Abbey smiled. 'Yeah. I dash home and milk with the mobile phone beside me and I dash back if needed. The locals are accustomed to the smell of cow dung mixed with antibiotic, and the cows have learned to be a bit negotiable in their milking times.'

'You're kidding,' Ryan said faintly. 'Abbey, what sort of life is that for a...?' He had been going to say a girl. And then Ryan looked down at Abbey's work-worn hands and corrected himself. 'For a woman?'

'It's my life.' Abbey sighed and smiled again. 'Well, maybe it's not for a while. It's now your life for a week— or at least the medical part is. After that, though, then it'll be my life ever after. I don't ask for anything more. Now... If you would, I would like you to take me home.'

'Abbey...' Ryan looked down at the white-faced girl in the wheelchair. She was still dressed in the stained shorts and T-shirt she'd worn all day. She looked weary beyond belief, in pain and looking to a future that held nothing but hard work.

And something twisted inside Ryan that hadn't been twisted in a long time. Something deep and strong and urgent.

It was only that he felt sorry for her, he told himself harshly, but he found his hand wandering to touch Abbey's dusky curls.

'You're hurting.'

'Just take me home, Ryan,' Abbey said. 'Ted can't drive or I'd ask him to take me.'

'Stay here,' he said.

'I can't.'

'You should be in hospital yourself.' Ryan let his fingers drift though her curls. Absently. Almost as if he wasn't noticing what he was doing. But he was noticing. He was very definitely noticing. The touch was doing strange things to his insides.

'And where would that leave Jack and Janet?' Abbey demanded, ignoring the feel of Ryan's fingers. Or trying to ignore them. 'I have to milk in the morning.'

'I'll do that.'

'You can't.'

'If you can do it,' Ryan said gently, 'so can I. You just said that your life is mine for a week. That includes your cows.'

'It's not necessary.'

'It is.'

'Ryan...'

'Look, I'm a country boy from way back,' Ryan told her, exasperated. 'I can milk a cow and I have your medical training. This is my honeymoon you're supposed to be on, Dr Wittner. I don't offer every girl a honeymoon. So I suggest you just take yourself to bed and get on with it.'

If only she could.

Abbey looked up into Ryan's face and thought of the impossibility of doing what he'd suggested. Taking a honeymoon.

Taking a holiday.

'Work never stops,' she said wearily. 'Never. Don't you know that, Ryan Henry?'

'It does, Abbey,' he said gently. 'It must.'

Only it didn't. It hadn't even now. Before Ryan finished speaking there was an urgent screech of brakes outside the casualty entrance. Three seconds later the glass doors opened and a young man burst in. He looked wildly around, dishevelled and frantic, and his eyes focussed on Ryan.

'Quick. Oh, please, come quick. Tessa's having a baby.'

She'll have to go to Cairns.'

'Nonsense.'

Outside the labour ward Ryan and Abbey were neck deep in argument. Inside, Tessa Ludlow was neck deep in labour.

'Hell, Abbey, I can't deliver her here.'

'She'll deliver herself, then. For heaven's sake, Ryan, all you have to do is go in there, check dilatation, check the foetal heart and stand around to catch. In fact, Sister's probably done all the busy work for you while you're hanging around here, procrastinating.'

Ryan raked his fingers through his hair. It was true. He was procrastinating. With good reason!

'Abbey, I'm a surgeon. An orthopaedic surgeon. How many babies do you think I've delivered?'

'They don't let you through medical school unless you've delivered a few,' Abbey said firmly. 'Unless US training is very different to what it is here.'

'But that was years ago. I haven't delivered a baby since.'

'It's what you said about milking—it's like riding a bicycle,' Abbey said promptly. 'Once learned, never forgotten. Nothing's changed. Unless I'm very much mistaken, babies still come out just the same way they did a hundred years ago. Ryan, get in there and deliver that baby.'

'But I'm not even registered here.' Ryan gave a sound that was practically a moan. 'Abbey, if something goes wrong I can get sued for millions.'

'You know, if something does go wrong and you're standing out here in the corridor, arguing about money, then you could be sued for even more!'

'Abbey…'

Abbey sighed. And took a deep breath. 'What is it? You want me to deliver the baby, Ryan? Is that what you're saying? Your offer was for the easy stuff only? Well, I guess I can reach the bed from the wheelchair if I really try. Maybe if you hold me up under my arms…'

Ryan glared.

'Go on, Ryan.' Abbey managed a smile. 'You remember that day you wanted your tooth to come out so you could spend your tooth-fairy money at the fête the next day? It was wobbly—but only just.'

'What on earth…?'

'You showed determination then.'

'Abbey, I must have been all of ten years old.'

'No difference,' Abbey said blithely. 'You tied yourself up with string and then made me slam the door. And you didn't even yell. Come on, Ryan, that's the stuff you're made of. Where's your determination now?'

The labour ward door opened. The night sister stood, gazing from one doctor to the other in exasperation.

'Have you two sorted out who's delivering this baby yet?' she asked sternly. 'Because if you don't figure it out soon I'm going to get all the credit. And that'd never do, now would it, Doctors?'

She winked at Abbey.

Ryan gave another groan, rolled up his sleeves—both metaphorically and physically—and went to deliver a baby.

In fact, it wasn't as easy as Abbey had foreseen.

Second stage took far too long. It was a first-time birth. The young mother was exhausted and frightened and it took all Ryan's bedside skills to calm her. Ryan finally effected a safe delivery, but only after applying forceps.

Funny that he remembered how. Abbey was right. It was like riding a bicycle.

Or like loving Abbey.

The thought flashed into Ryan's mind as he stared down at the red and yowling infant in his hands, and he found himself smiling at the thought. Abbey had bullied him into delivering this baby and, to his astonishment, he'd found the experience deeply satisfying. Tessa and her husband were gazing at him as if he'd just personally produced their miracle, and the baby was warm and healthy and full of new life in his hands.

How many times in the past had Abbey bullied him into doing something he'd loved once he'd tried? 'Come on, Ryan. Take your shoes off. You can't catch crabs properly unless your toes ooze mud...'

Ryan inserted a few neat stitches in Tessa's perineum, checked his baby over thoroughly—odd how it felt like his—and, with a chest expanded a few inches from an hour ago, went to find Abbey.

She was curled up on a couch in the waiting room in Casualty, and she was fast asleep.

Ryan stared down at Abbey for a long, long moment.

The same Abbey. She looked a real waif here. Dirty, bedraggled and her leg in the huge white dressing...

His mother had called her trash.

Abbey was no such thing.

Abbey was *some* lady, Ryan conceded, staring down at her in wonder. She was a lady with iron determination and courage to match her heart. A friend to be proud of.

What would his life have been if he'd stayed at Sapphire Cove? Ryan found himself wondering. In the background he heard his newly delivered baby start to cry. A nurse moved swiftly down the corridor. There were coos and chuckles and a low conversation between the young father and the nurse.

They all knew each other here.

This hospital was about as different from the hospital where Ryan worked as he could possibly get.

He'd go crazy working for a week here, he told himself. No research. No colleagues, bouncing ideas off each other. No social life outside the hospital. No concerts, art galleries or restaurants. How could Abbey stand it?

He looked down at the sleeping girl on the couch and a shaft of pain shot through him—a pain so fierce he almost staggered. A pain of sheer, absolute want. He wanted to gather her to him. Protect her from the pain he saw on her face. Take a load off her shoulders that seemed too heavy for any woman to bear.

It wasn't on. This was crazy thinking. Ryan wasn't about to walk away from a fantastic career and lifestyle just because he was being sentimental about an old friend.

There was a soft step behind him. Ryan turned to see Ted lurking in the doorway. Ghoul-like.

'She looks at death's door,' Ted said with a certain amount of relish. 'You're not going to take her home now, are you, Doc?'

'She'll fight me if I don't.'

'Seems to me there's not a lot of fight left in her,' Ted said morosely. 'Now, if I was a young fella I'd just gather her up and take her to bed.' Then he coloured. 'I mean…put her to bed, like…'

Ryan smiled.

He turned to look down at Abbey and his smile faded. A sudden image of what that might be like pierced his senses. To take Abbey to bed…

No way. That was the last thing he needed. The last thing Abbey needed. He was an engaged man. Abbey had responsibilities.

Bed, pure and simple—bed in the old-fashioned sense—was what this lady needed. With a wrench, Ryan forced his mind to practicalities.

'Will Janet cope if Abbey doesn't come home?' he asked dubiously.

'I've already rung Janet,' Ted told him. 'When I found our Doc Wittner asleep, like. She won't worry. Janet's a good 'un.'

'But the baby… And I've told her I'll do the milking but she'll panic…'

'Janet says young Jack's asleep. Janet can cope with the little 'un's breakfast, and the milking don't need to get done again till morning,' Ted told him. 'And I've got ideas about that. So let's worry about the morning in the morning. Sister's got a bed made up in Room Four for Doc Wittner and one in Room Seven for you. So go tuck her in and then hit the sack yourself.' He eyed Ryan shrewdly. 'Looks to me you need a bit of shut-eye almost as much as Doc Wittner.'

He did, Ryan acknowledged.

The pressures of the day were crowding in, threatening to overwhelm him. With the time change in international travel, he'd missed two nights' sleep. He'd hit Abbey's bicycle and hurt Abbey. He'd coped with his father's heart attack. He'd delivered a baby.

It was time to call it quits and do as he was told. But first…

He nodded acknowledgement to Ted, and stooped to lift Abbey into his arms. She was feather-light—far too slim for a woman of her age. He half expected her to wake when he lifted her, but the after-effects of the morphine and shock from the accident were taking their toll. There was no argument from Abbey. She sighed in her sleep and nestled easily into his arms, her breasts moulding themselves against his chest as if she were meant to lie there. As if she were part of him...

Ryan strode down the corridor with his sleeping burden, knowing that things were changing inside him that he had no idea how to set right again.

Worry about it in the morning, he told himself firmly. These feelings...the feel of Abbey against him...the trace of perfume in her hair...the way her breasts curved in against him as she lay in his arms in total trust... What he was feeling was just a result of a crazy two days.

He had to sleep. In the morning he could go back to being Ryan Henry, hugely successful orthopaedic surgeon and future husband to Felicity, all over again.

In the morning...

CHAPTER FIVE

ABBEY woke to breakfast.

There was a smell of bacon, wafting around her, and her nose twitched in appreciation before she opened her eyes. When she did lift a cautious eyelid the first thing she saw was a breakfast tray.

The second was Ryan Henry.

'Well, well.' Ryan was lifting the lid from her eggs and bacon and nodding his approval of what lay underneath. 'You've decided to join the land of the living. Excellent. I'd have let you sleep longer but I wanted to bully you into breakfast before clinic. I've heard you should always eat a big breakfast on the first day of your honeymoon. It's medically recommended.'

'I... You...' Abbey winced and stirred—and then stared. This was crazy. Last night she'd settled down on a couch in the waiting room. Now... She cast a wary glance at Ryan and then cautiously lifted her bedclothes.

And yelped.

'Is something wrong?' Ryan enquired blandly.

'My clothes...' Abbey hauled her bedcovers up to her nose and glared. 'What happened to my clothes?'

'You sound as if you're naked,' Ryan complained. 'Which, considering the amount of trouble Sister and I had getting you into a hospital gown, is a tad unappreciative. I know for a honeymoon you really should have something sheer and sexy—preferably black—but I'm afraid hospital green was all we could come up with.'

Abbey was no longer listening. She couldn't care less what she was wearing. It was the identity of the person who'd dressed her—or rather who'd *undressed* her—that was important here.

67

'Sister dressed me?' she asked cautiously, sitting up with her bedclothes still up to her neck.

'I helped, but only as far as was decent.' Ryan smiled. 'You don't remember? Your clothes were disgusting. I was afraid they'd infect your scratches if we left you in them any longer.'

'My T-shirt...'

'I didn't like it,' Ryan said, as if that clinched the matter. 'And your shorts were torn already.'

'What have you done with my T-shirt and shorts?' Abbey demanded in a voice that was loaded with portent. For answer, Ryan pointed to a pair of scissors on the bed-side table.

'All gone.' It was an imitation of Ted's voice that he used when discussing a death. Full of ghoul-like relish. 'We disturbed you less by cutting them off. Ted took 'em away to use as dusters down in the morgue. We figured that's the best place for them. Now, if I were you, I'd eat some breakfast before it gets cold. Considering the amount of trouble Cook's gone to on your behalf, letting this lot get cold would be a real shame.'

'Ryan, I want my clothes.'

'They're in a million pieces.' Ryan handed her a slice of toast. 'Bite.'

Abbey bit. And glared.

'Problem?' Ryan enquired politely. He stood back with his arms folded and watched her—doctor watching inter-esting specimen. Ryan was dressed in fresh trousers and an open-necked, short-sleeved shirt. His wavy brown hair was neatly brushed. He looked like he'd had about twelve hours sleep instead of a scant six and he was showered and freshly shaved. Ryan Henry was a doctor in charge of his world again.

Which Abbey definitely wasn't.

However, she *was* hungry. She bit into her toast once more, trying to get her thoughts in order. There'd been Janet's casserole last night, but she'd eaten hardly any before they'd been called to help Sam. And the smell was fabulous.

'What are you going to do about my clothes?' It was tricky to talk with a mouthful of toast when one was concentrating on glaring at the same time, but Abbey managed it, no sweat.

'Nothing,' Ryan told her. 'They were appalling. They certainly don't deserve burial honours, if that's what you're suggesting.'

Abbey didn't smile. She concentrated fiercely on her breakfast, not looking at Ryan. For some reason, the sight of Ryan Henry standing beside her bed, surveying her with an air of proprietary interest, unnerved her completely. Abbey lifted a piece of bacon and inspected it from all angles. And decided not to take offence at the bacon. In it went. 'They were the only clothes I have,' she said between mouthfuls.

'Surely not!' Ryan's eyebrows rose in polite disbelief. 'Abbey, I know you're poor, but I find it hard to believe you spend your entire life as a doctor, a farmer and a mother dressed in the one T-shirt.'

'OK, smarty-boots!' Abbey glowered. 'I meant they were the only clothes I have here. Ryan, you were supposed to take me home.'

'You passed out before I could. I never send unconscious patients home. It's against medical ethics. And you've been unconscious for over twelve hours.'

'I was asleep. You knew very well I was just asleep.' Abbey lifted a fork and attacked her egg—and then paused with her fork halfway to her mouth. 'Did you say *twelve hours*?' She swivelled to look at the bedside clock. And gasped. 'Nine... Oh, glory, it's nine o'clock. Ryan, how could you?' Her fork clattered onto her plate, forgotten, and her legs swung sideways.

To be blocked by Ryan.

'So, where do you think you're going?'

'Home,' Abbey said in a distressed voice. 'Ryan, it's nine o'clock. The cows will be frantic and Janet will try to milk them herself and there's no one to look after Jack while she does, even if she could manage the milking, and—'

'Ted's organised your cows.'

'Ted…'

'I intended to milk them but Ted tells me there's any number of local farmers willing to roster themselves to milk your herd,' Ryan said. His hands moved to her shoulders and he held her still, brooking no argument. 'Ted says the locals think the world of you. If you need help, all you have to do is ask. This morning Ted asked on your behalf. He was inundated with offers.'

'No!' Abbey's face creased in distress. 'I won't ask for help. Everyone did so much. When John died… When he was in the coma… I was pregnant and they helped so much. Everyone helped. I don't need help any more. We can stand on our own feet.'

'You mean you don't need their help ever again?' Ryan asked.

'No. I don't. I won't.'

'Yet Ted tells me there's not a person living within a thirty-mile radius of Sapphire Cove who doesn't use *your* help,' Ryan said thoughtfully. 'You do house calls at all hours. You've bullied the government into subsidies so this hospital could be built. You've given the community medical treatment that's never been available before. Ted says you give and give and give—and everyone wants desperately to give something back. What's the old adage here, Abbey? It's better to give than receive? Well, sometimes it's only fair to let the giving be both ways.'

'You don't understand.' Abbey shook her head and pushed her tousled curls back from her face. 'Janet will—'

'I've talked to Janet,' Ryan told her. 'I was out there an hour ago, checking everything was going OK. I've told her I'm keeping you in hospital today to give that leg a chance to settle. If you're good then you can go home tomorrow. I've organised Marcia over the road to come and give Janet a hand with Jack—if necessary she'll do that for the next week so you can rest—and the local farmers are arranging a roster system with the milking until your leg's OK. Until *I say* your leg's OK. And Janet…'

'Janet will hate it.'

'She was upset,' Ryan admitted, 'but I told her your health was at stake. I gave her the same lecture about giving and receiving as I gave you and she's content.'

'She'd never agree…'

'She has.'

'I don't believe you.'

But Ryan wasn't listening. He'd picked up the bedside phone and was dialling. 'Let her tell you herself. Don't believe me, oh ye of little faith. Talk to Janet.'

And thirty seconds later Abbey replaced the receiver and stared up at Ryan, totally bewildered.

'I don't know how you did that.'

'Pure charm.' Ryan smiled his most enigmatic smile and pointed to Abbey's breakfast. 'Now eat.' He hauled a chair up and sat himself down—a man at ease with his world. 'There are things I need help with now, Abbey. Just keep eating while I fire questions.'

'Like?'

'I'm not asking anything while you're not eating.'

'OK. OK. I'm eating.' Abbey shoved a mouthful of egg home and frowned. 'I don't understand any of this. You can't just organise my life.'

'It's not your life now,' Ryan pointed out. 'We made a bargain. I drove too fast, I hurt your leg and I'm paying. You're on my honeymoon. I'm on your duties. You…'

But Abbey was no longer listening. Another anxiety had just crowded in. 'Ryan, how's Sam? How's your father?' It was a fast change of tack but it was the way Abbey's mind was working. Leapfrogging from one worry to another.

'Dad's OK.' Ryan's air of a man in charge slipped a little. 'I have the feeling what happened last night was crescendo angina, rather than a full-blown heart attack, as he's

settled fast, but the damage that's already been done...
Well, I wish I could say he's fine but he's holding his own.'

'He needs by-pass surgery, and he needs it now.'

'He won't go. I pushed it this morning—'

'How long have you been up?' Abbey demanded, off on
another track, and Ryan shrugged.

'Since five. I gave our jellyfish victim more morphine at
five. The pain takes a long time to wear off from those
damned things. After that it was hardly worth going back
to bed. My father was awake so we talked.'

'About by-passes?'

'That and other things. He won't do it.'

Abbey nodded. 'I told you, Ryan. He wants to die.'

'That's crazy.'

'It's not crazy. Think about it. All he has is a son who
hasn't been near him for seventeen years.'

'Oh, for heaven's sake...'

Abbey shook her head as she saw the rigid look on
Ryan's face. 'OK. I know. This is none of my business.
Apart from your father, tell me what else you need help
with.'

Ryan's set look eased a little. 'Did I say needed help?'

'Yes, you did and it floored me,' Abbey said bluntly.
'The great Ryan Henry, needing help!'

Ryan's anger gave way to bewilderment at the sudden
laughter in Abbey's eyes. If there was one thing he was
unaccustomed to, it was being teased. He shook his head.
'Abbey, for some reason... Am I wrong, or am I getting
the impression that you think I'm an autocratic, self-
opinionated—'

'Yep. All of the above.'

'I'm not.'

'No? I suppose you're a really thoughtful, considerate
human being.'

'I might be.'

'Well, if you're so thoughtful, you didn't by any
chance...' Abbey cast him a hopeful look '...bring me
some clothes when you went out to see Janet?'

'Nope.'

'There you are, then. Autocratic, unfeeling, inconsiderate…'

Ryan sighed. He and Abbey seemed destined to spend the morning sparring. 'OK, Abbey. Enough. Just fill me in on a few histories here. I need a verbal changeover. Your patient notes are nigh on unintelligible.'

'I guess that's because I'm the only one who ever reads them,' Abbey admitted contritely. 'I'm not used to handing over. Tell you what. Find me some clothes and I'll do a ward round with you and hand over personally.'

'You're not getting dressed. And you're not going anywhere.'

'Ryan…'

'No.'

'What if I stay in a wheelchair?' Abbey said meekly. 'And promise to act subservient all the time.'

'Abbey…'

'Please?' She smiled, and her smile lit up her eyes. It really was the loveliest smile.

Ryan caved in. He always had.

He stared down at her, baulked and baffled, and then he sighed. 'OK, Abbey. Ten minutes. I'll bring a wheelchair and a dressing-gown back here in ten minutes but if you haven't eaten every scrap of your breakfast you're not going anywhere.'

'Yes, sir!'

Sapphire Cove Bush Nursing Hospital boasted fifteen beds, twelve of which were full. Four of those were nursing home patients, which left eight acute cases to discuss. All eight patients were agog to see their accustomed doctor being pushed around in a wheelchair, her bandaged leg stuck straight out before her on a support board—and being propelled by a man many of them vaguely recognised from almost twenty years ago.

'Ryan Henry…' Old Mr Thomlinson gave a wheezy

chuckle and held out his hand in greeting. 'Well, well. Back in your old partnership, I see.'

'Partnership?'

'You and Abbey.' Bert Thomlinson looked from Ryan down to Abbey and grinned at the memory. 'Caught the pair of you swimming out to the reef and pinching crayfish from my traps when you were about twelve and eight years old apiece. Like two little fish, you were, diving down and hauling crays out of the trap. You were letting the little ones go, you told me, and gave me a lecture on catching babies.' He chortled. 'At the time I felt like tanning the hides of the pair of you, but you know what? I've never kept an undersized lobster since.' He broke into a fit of coughing and Abbey clucked reproof.

'That's what you get for telling tales out of school, Bert Thomlinson.' She looked up at Ryan. 'Bert's recovering from two nasty patches of pneumonia affecting both lungs. Caught, no doubt, from going fishing late at night and not getting out of wet clothes. And I don't believe you've re-formed, Bert. I'll bet you were still catching undersized crays.'

'I never would,' Bert said, wounded. 'The look of you back then, Abbey... No higher than my waist, standing there with your fingers all bloody from getting nipped and making me sound like a child murderer for catching baby crays. And young Ryan standing in front of you, ready to defend you to the death...' He fell back on his pillows and smiled. 'Well, it does me good to see the pair of you back together again, even if it took a busted leg to do it.'

That was pretty much the opinion of the entire older population of the hospital. Ryan found he was recognised with real pleasure, and he also discovered that he liked the sensation. Very much.

The best greeting, though, was from his father. Ryan only had to walk into his father's room for the old man's eyes to light up with delight.

Double delight when he saw Abbey.

'How's the leg?' Sam demanded, reaching out and gripping Ryan's hand between his attached tubes. Abbey saw the gesture with resignation. Did Ryan really not realise how much his father loved him? Did he really not realise that Sam needed a lot more than duty letters from his beloved son?

'Better than your heart. Sam, you have to get this bypass,' Abbey said bluntly.

'So Ryan says. But there's no *have to* about it. It's my heart. I can do what I like with it.'

'Like let it stop?'

'Abbey…'

Abbey took a deep breath. She glanced uncertainly up at Ryan and then turned her attention solely to Ryan's father. And took a chance…

'Sam, would it help if Ryan told you he'll look after your farm while you have the operation, and that he'll stay until you're on the mend again?'

Silence.

Ryan said nothing.

That didn't mean Ryan's mind wasn't working, though. Good grief. What was Abbey saying? Abbey was just committing him here. Committing him to stay here for a month or more.

'But…Abbey, I can't…' he said blankly.

'Of course you can't.' Sam's voice was tired, and bleak, and absolutely final. 'That's stupid, Abbey. Ryan has his career back in the USA. He just can't dump it to look after me. And he has this lady—Felicity isn't it, son? Felicity won't want to stick around here with a sick old man.'

Felicity wouldn't. Of course she wouldn't. Felicity was an oncologist—a cancer specialist—as expert in her field as Ryan was in his. She'd had trouble slotting a honeymoon into her busy schedule anyway. To extend the honeymoon for a few weeks…

Impossible. Impossible for both of them. Felicity was needed back at work as much as Ryan.

But Sam was fading back into the pillows and his grip on Ryan's hand had eased. It was as if, for a brief moment,

Sam had allowed himself to show his need for his son, and now he was schooling himself to let go.

And Abbey's face was absolutely expressionless.

Ryan's gut tightened. Hell, there was only so much of this a man could take. It was an impossible thing to ask. It was impossible to stay. But… With Sam's hand in his and Abbey looking at him like that… It was impossible for him to go.

'I meant I can't see why not,' Ryan said strongly—roughly—and his hand tightened on his father's, re-establishing the link. Re-establishing the need. 'I can keep up with my research work over here. There's articles I need to write up and I have my lap-top computer with me. I have everything I need.'

Of course he had his lap-top with him. To go on a honeymoon without work was unthinkable.

To stay away from work for more than two weeks was unthinkable. The reorganisation that would have to be done was unbelievable. And there was Richard Crogin to worry about. Richard was after Ryan's job, and if Ryan was away…

But suddenly all that mattered was the link between his father's hand and his—and the luminous glow that was beaming straight up at him from Abbey.

'You mean it?' Abbey asked breathlessly. 'Oh, Ryan…'

Ryan's resolution firmed.

'Of course I mean it.' He looked down at his father. 'If you agree to the surgery then I'll stay for at least a month.'

Sam blinked. He looked up at his son in bewilderment, and Abbey felt her delight fade. Maybe it wasn't enough. Abbey's own heart sank. For Ryan to promise a month… There was nothing promised for the end of that month. There was no commitment to a future for the old man in that. One month, a couple of weeks of which Sam would spend in hospital in Cairns…

Maybe Sam still wouldn't agree.

But Sam was looking from Ryan to Abbey with eyes that were lightening by the minute. There was a spark of interest glowing in their depths that Abbey hadn't seen for years.

'What about your Felicity?' Sam asked his son.

'I'll talk to Felicity,' Ryan said heavily. 'We might have to reorganise things.'

'Put the wedding off?'

'I don't know.' Was Ryan imagining it or was there a tiny hopeful note behind Sam's words? 'I'll have to talk to her. Maybe she'll come out, we'll get married and she'll go back before me.' That might be the best plan. Then, again, Felicity might decide she wanted a real honeymoon and put everything off until they could take more time away together. Which would be a year or more from now.

It didn't matter.

The thought of a delay to their wedding—and its seeming irrelevance—made Ryan frown. It didn't matter if their wedding was put off? Why?

Never mind. He could think of Felicity later. For now there was his father's agreement to gain. His father's health. That was the important thing. That was why he didn't have room to worry about Felicity.

There couldn't be any other reason.

'You need to agree, Dad,' he said, and met his father's eyes directly. 'I want you to have this surgery. The way your heart is now—well, you could have a full-blown heart attack at any minute and you could die. And I badly don't want that to happen.'

'You meant that?'

'Of course I mean it.' And he did. For twenty years Ryan had been carrying the look of his father as he and his mother had boarded the plane away from here. His father's look had been blank, expressionless, and—Ryan had thought—uncaring.

Abbey had told him that he was wrong to believe his father uncaring. And suddenly he believed Abbey.

His father loved him and it was a damned good feeling. He didn't want to lose that. He didn't want to lose Sam now, when he had just discovered that he had a father after

all. A real father. Not a pen at the end of a series of duty
letters.

And Sam was looking from Abbey to Ryan and back
again.

And smiling.

'Well, I guess I'd better have that surgery after all,' he
whispered. 'You say you'll stay a month?'

'A month.'

'Well, anything can happen in a month,' Sam said am-
biguously. 'It's worth taking a risk on.'

Abbey didn't see Ryan again for another few hours. He
settled her back into bed—once more refusing her request
for clothes—and gave instructions for the nursing staff not
to let her out of bed. Then he took himself off to do her
clinic. Ryan came back into the hospital at eleven when the
ambulance arrived to transport his father to Cairns, but by
then Abbey was dead to the world.

It was as if Abbey's exhaustion of the last few months—
or maybe the last few years—had finally caught up with
her. That, and the shock of the accident the day before, let
her sleep the sleep of the dead. Janet and Jack and her cows
and farm were in safe hands. Her clinic was in Ryan's
hands. Sam was having his by-pass.

For once all was right with her world. She slept.

She woke briefly at lunch to find Eileen hovering over
her with orders to see she ate every mouthful, and then she
slept again. When she woke once more Ryan was standing
over her bed, smiling down at her with satisfaction.

'If you don't wake up soon you'll miss bedtime,' he
warned, and Abbey managed a sleepy smile.

'It can't be bedtime. No one's bullied me into dinner
yet.'

Ryan looked at his watch. 'You're right. It's five-thirty.
Dinner at six and bedtime at seven.'

Abbey nodded. The idea had immediate appeal. 'I don't
know why I'm doing this,' she murmured. 'It's not like I
was really hurt yesterday.'

'No? You're telling me you're not aching in every bone in your body? Truly, Abbey?'

Abbey stirred and checked herself out. Every bone? Well, maybe. Every bone certainly complained.

'Yeah, well, it's only bruising.'

'I know.' Ryan touched her lightly on the cheek—a touch that sent Abbey's senses screaming. 'Plus the fact that you're exhausted.' He hauled a chair over and sat down. 'Abbey, you can't keep going like this,' he said gently. 'I've seen your medical workload now. This community needs two doctors—or at least one and a half. And, with Jack to care for and the farm to run, you should be the half.'

'No.' Abbey shook her head with decision. 'No way.'

'Because someone else would take over some of the limelight? Because you like being the town's only doctor?'

'That's unfair,' Abbey said firmly. 'Ryan, I'd let go if I could, but finding another doctor to move to a rural area...'

'Even an area as beautiful as Sapphire Cove?'

'Doctors want big hospitals and specialists on call and private schools and universities on tap for their children,' Abbey told him. 'I thought your mother would have drilled into you what an unsuitable place Sapphire Cove is to live. I shouldn't have to.'

She had. Ryan flinched.

'But even so, Abbey...'

'Even so, I can't afford to work less. I have debts.'

'John's debts?'

'That's none of your business.'

'Maybe, but I had a talk to one of your patients this afternoon,' Ryan told her. 'Mr Ellis. The local bank manager. He came in with shingles.'

'Shingles...' Abbey screwed up her nose, her attention diverted. 'Oh, no. The poor man. Shingles is so painful. Did you start him on acyclovir?' She pushed herself up on her pillows. 'Ryan, it'll be a new treatment since you trained. You must start him on that in the first twenty-four hours. It really does stop shingles in its tracks—quarters the time of discomfort. If you haven't been around as a general practitioner for—'

'I know all about acyclovir,' Ryan told her, and then smiled at her look of disbelief. 'Don't worry. I know I'm out of touch with general practice but I've figured a really efficient way of sounding as if I know what I'm talking about while I'm seeing your patients. I've hooked up to the Internet. On the Internet I can play doctor-patient in a virtual hospital. All I have to do is type 'shingles' and out comes all the latest treatments and references to all the current literature. Excerpts and précis included.'

'You mean you leave the patient—'

'I have my lap-top computer on my desk,' he told her smugly. 'I tell the patient I'm recording details of their case as I go, and all the time I'm asking what the heck the latest treatment for shingles is. Then I do a fast search of *Mims*— on compact disc—and I find the drug dosages and brand names and everything I need to make myself sound intelligent.

'Oh, and by the way.' He smiled. 'In case you were worrying, I rang the medical board and they've given me emergency registration as an interim measure.'

'Oh, Ryan...' Abbey's hand flew up to her mouth. 'I forgot.'

'Understandable.' He smiled again, his lazy, caring smile that ran right through her. 'You're not well, Abbey. And not just because of the accident. You've run yourself into the ground. And Mr Ellis says—'

'You shouldn't have been discussing me with my bank manager,' Abbey said fretfully, and Ryan shook his head.

'I haven't been discussing you with anyone. I've simply been listening while one patient after another has come in, berated me for knocking you off your bicycle and then told me how worried they are about you. And Mr Ellis has done more than that. He tells me the debts you're paying off are gambling debts incurred when John was under such pressure he didn't know what he was doing. He says he's advised you strongly to declare yourself bankrupt, wipe the slate clean and start again.'

'How can I do that?'

'Simple. Find yourself a lawyer and do it. He also said you can't lose the farm. Your home's exempt and, with Janet and Jack living there, too, it's doubly insured. He said you could have stayed living where you were.'

'And have Jack growing up with people knowing his father owed them money he never repaid,' Abbey said simply. 'No, thank you. This is my problem, Ryan, and I'll thank you to butt out of it.' She swallowed but the expression on her face of grim determination didn't waver. 'Who…who else did you see in clinic?'

And Ryan stared down, baffled. It had seemed so simple when Brian Ellis had explained it to him. Abbey should declare herself bankrupt, get rid of her debts and then find another doctor to take over at least half her workload. And Ryan could walk away with a clear conscience.

Not yet he couldn't. Not for a month…

But at the end of the month? When his father was recovered from his surgery? Ryan wanted to be able to walk away from here, knowing that his friend's security was assured. And how could he do that if she was going to be obstinate and proud and stubborn as a mule?

But he didn't want her any other way.

'Tell me who else you saw in clinic,' Abbey insisted, and Ryan blinked. He wasn't used to this. He was accustomed to being in charge. To people coming to him when they were in trouble and demanding his help. Well, Abbey had accepted his help—albeit grudgingly—for a week, but not after that. And he found himself thinking how impossible it would be to live with himself, knowing he'd left her like this. Burdened with work. Burdened with debt and responsibility.

'As I said, most cases I found I could handle,' he told her, forcing his mind back to the patients he'd seen. 'I had old Angus Harvey with an infection on his penis. Walked in and said—straight-faced, ''Doc, there's a ring round me old bloke and it ain't lipstick''! That was the hardest part of my day, trying to keep a straight face and treat his infection at the same time...'

'You sound like you enjoyed it,' Abbey said wonderingly, and Ryan grinned.

'To tell you the truth, I did. Oh, and I saw Mrs Miller. She came in to get her ulcer dressed again.' He shook his head. 'She must just like doctors, Abbey. The ulcer didn't need dressing.'

'Did you ask her what was worrying her?' Abbey asked anxiously, and Ryan frowned.

'I told you. She wanted her ulcer dressed.'

'And I told you, there's something else troubling Marg Miller.' Abbey shook her head. 'Men! You have no intuition at all. It's not her ulcer she's worried about. It's her son. There's something wrong with Ian. I'm sure of it. Mrs Miller wouldn't worry like this for herself. He must be in some sort of trouble.'

'Her son...' Ryan frowned. 'Ian Miller. I think I remember him. He's my age—a bit older.'

'That's right. He's living in Sydney.'

'And you think he might be ill?'

'I have no idea,' Abbey said with asperity. 'If you'd asked, you might have found out.'

'Ian's not my patient.'

'He's not mine either. I haven't seen him for years. But his well-being is affecting my patient and therefore I worry. That's what a good general practitioner does.'

'I wouldn't know,' Ryan said dryly. 'I'm an orthopaedic surgeon, remember.' He paused, waiting for comment. Waiting for Abbey to apologise.

No apology was forthcoming.

The silence stretched out to an embarrassing length. Clearly Abbey's opinion of orthopaedic surgeons—or one orthopedic surgeon in particular—was less than flattering.

'I'll telephone her,' Abbey said at last.

'No.' Ryan shook his head. 'If you really think there's

something happening that's serious then I'll telephone and talk to her again.'

'You wouldn't consider going out there and talking to her face to face?'

'Abbey!' Ryan said explosively. 'Don't push me…'

'I can only try.' She ventured a teasing grin. 'And you can only say no.'

'I'll go if I have time, but I will telephone,' Ryan promised, a man driven against the ropes. He sighed. 'And you might like to know Janet's agreed for me to replace her hip next Monday. I can organise it by then.'

'Next…' Abbey stared. 'You mean you *will* do it?'

'I said I'd do it. Why should you doubt me?'

'But next Monday…' Abbey frowned. 'Ryan, it's only Monday now. That's a whole week away. I'll be back working by then.'

'No, you won't,' Ryan said roughly. 'There's been a change in plan. Janet will need at least three weeks before she can think of looking after Jack again. So…you stay home full time and look after Jack for two weeks and I organise help. We need help for me for the next two weeks and then for you when Sam comes home from hospital.'

'Help?' Abbey shook her head, dazed.

'There's a locum arriving tomorrow. Steve Pryor. I've rung a few contacts in Brisbane and they tell me he's good. We're lucky he's free at short notice.'

Disregarding her aching bones, Abbey sat up in bed with a jolt. 'Ryan Henry, you can't do this. I can't afford—'

'No, but I can.'

'But I *can't*!'

'Abbey, it's my job I'm sharing for a bit here,' Ryan reminded her, 'not yours.'

'You agreed to work the week.'

'Yes,' Ryan agreed, his voice gentling. 'And I'm not going back on that promise. 'I promised to look after your practice for a week. But Dad's surgery is scheduled for the day after tomorrow and I want to be in Cairns during his operation. And maybe for twenty-four hours afterwards.'

'Oh, Ryan...' Abbey's face creased in distress. 'Of course. I didn't think of that. But I can look after things. By the day after tomorrow—'

'I've organised tomorrow, too,' Ryan said blandly. 'About my honeymoon...'

'Ryan—'

'Just shut up and listen,' he told her in a voice that brooked no argument. 'Abbey, there is no need for you to get your knickers in a knot about my arrangements. Tomorrow I'm taking you out of here and driving you to your honeymoon destination.'

'Honeymoon...' Abbey stared. She was starting to feel as if her world was tilting sideways on its axis. And any minute now she'd fall right off.

'Well, Felicity and I weren't intending to stay with Dad for our honeymoon,' Ryan told her. 'Felicity organised us a place on the beach ten minutes' drive from here. That's where you're going. Tomorrow.'

'But, Ryan, even if I could, I don't want to,' Abbey wailed. 'I want my little Jack. I want Janet.'

'Now, how did I know you'd say that?' Ryan grinned. 'That's all organised. I agree with you that Janet could use a rest as well as you and I'd like her fit to face surgery. So I rang the owners of the place we booked and they've swapped the booking from a one-bedroom to a two-bedroom unit. So...I've given the same ultimatum to Janet as I give to you. Pack and be ready for your honeymoon by tomorrow morning or I'll pick you up and take you in what you're wearing at the time.' His grin deepened. 'And I mean that, Abbey Wittner.'

Then his grin faded at the look of dazed incredulity on Abbey's face. 'What's wrong?' To Ryan's astonishment, Abbey's eyes were filling with tears. 'Abbey, for heaven's sake...'

'A holiday... You really mean a holiday?' Abbey choked. 'Ryan, I haven't had a holiday for years. You can't really mean... I don't deserve this.'

'I think you do, Abbey,' Ryan said quietly. He stooped

and kissed her on the cheek. His hand came down and
cupped the curve of her grazed and bandaged cheek, wiping
away an errant tear. 'If anyone deserves a honeymoon you
do—and it's all my pleasure to be able to give you one.'

And what Felicity would say when she realised he'd
given away the magic honeymoon destination she'd spent
days researching, he hated to think.

Felicity, however, seemed a very long way away.

Felicity was for tomorrow.

CHAPTER SIX

RYAN appeared at about nine the next morning with a youngish, scholarly man in tow. It didn't take a genius to work out this was Ryan's new locum. There was a stethoscope around the young man's neck and an owlish look of anxiety on his face.

Abbey wasn't in her ward. Ryan tracked her down in the children's ward.

'Why aren't you in bed?' Ryan glowered from the doorway and then relented enough to smile at the little girl in the bed. 'Hi, Leith. Still feeling better?'

Leith Kinley managed a wan smile. She was a regular here. A chronic asthmatic, she'd been admitted into hospital more times than Abbey could remember, and each time her attacks seemed to worsen.

At the other end of the hospital, Abbey had slept though Leith's admission last night, but the nurses had told her this morning that Ryan had had a hard time getting her stabilised.

Ryan had been up all night. Abbey wouldn't have thought it to look at him now. He seemed bright and alert and raring to go.

'Hey, Leith, I've brought another doctor for you to meet.'

Ryan gave Abbey a smile but he spoke directly to the little girl in the bed. Leith Kinley was terrified of her asthma attacks and, as Abbey watched the way Ryan treated her, she knew Ryan was aware of the child's terror. 'Leith, this is Dr Steve Pryor. Dr Pryor, this is Miss Leith Kinley and the lady beside her is an escapee from another ward, Dr Abbey Wittner.'

To Abbey's astonishment and pleasure, Steve Pryor leaned over and solemnly shook Leith's hand first.

Amazing! A locum who treated patients—even child patients—as humans. And greeted them on a needs basis.

Where on earth had Ryan found someone like Steve?

'Are you ready to go, Abbey?' Ryan's dangerous smile twinkled out. 'Or do I have to carry out my threat?'

'Despite your threats, I'm going nowhere in a hospital gown,' Abbey said with dignity, and Ryan nodded.

'Of course not. There's a dress on your bed. I chose it myself.'

'You chose a dress...'

'I mean, from your wardrobe,' he said sanguinely. 'Janet was busy supervising milking when I dropped in. You could go and put it on,' he added politely.

Then Ryan turned back to Leith. Ignoring everyone else, he stooped and took Leith's two little hands between his bigger ones while Abbey watched, still hornswoggled.

'Leith, I know last night's asthma attack scared you. It scared all of us. This morning I've been doing some hard thinking about how we can improve matters, and I've been talking to your mum and dad.'

This morning. Abbey glanced disbelievingly at her watch. Ryan had been up all night with an asthmatic child. He'd been out to the farm to find her a dress. Then he'd talked to an ill child's parents and finally found time to meet a new doctor. All this by nine o'clock. Also she'd heard Ryan doing a ward round at about seven.

'Your mum and dad agree that we need to do something more than just give you medicine,' Ryan was saying. 'Leith, we need to improve your lung capacity. Make your lungs bigger, if you like, so you can get more air.'

Leith frowned. 'How do I do that?' she whispered.

'Swimming,' Ryan said promptly. 'And, if you agree, your first swimming lesson is this morning. I'm taking Dr Wittner to the beach and, if you like, you can come too. You can have a gentle swim with me showing you what to do to build your lungs, and then I'll bring you back here.'

'I can't go home?'

'I'll bring you back to the hospital for lunch and a really

good sleep. Then, if your breathing is OK, your mum and dad will take you home tonight. And we've agreed that your mum and dad will take you swimming every day for a month. After a month we'll think about whether it's doing you good or not.'

Abbey stared. She'd suggested this. First rule for asthmatics was to attempt to increase lung capacity. But Leith had been reluctant to try swimming lessons and Leith's parents had always been adamant that they hadn't time.

Something had changed.

Ryan had said Leith's parents had agreed.

He'd bulldozed them, Abbey decided. He'd bulldozed them in the same way he bulldozed everyone else. He got his own way just by going in with force.

Well, it had worked. And something else had changed. Leith's reluctance. Leith was looking up at Ryan with a tremulous smile. 'I can go swimming with you now?'

'With me and with Dr Wittner. And maybe with Dr Wittner's baby, Jack, and Jack's grandma. Is that OK?' Ryan turned to Abbey and pointed to his watch. 'What are you hanging around here for, Dr Wittner? Be ready in five minutes or face the consequences.'

Ryan's honeymoon retreat was the kind of paradise Abbey had never dreamed of.

The sign at the end of the beach road simply said 'Bliss', the word painted with small black lettering on a cream sign and discreetly tucked in between the coconut palms. Abbey had heard of this place, but had never been here. Few locals had, and for one good reason.

They couldn't afford it.

From the time Ryan nosed his car into the wide, white sweep of the entrance the place screamed money at its most tasteful.

Reception was vast—a cavern of pale grey marble with great wooden ceiling fans, stirring the warm air straight from the sea, and huge cane chairs and settees with cushions that just begged to be sat on. The whole of Reception was open to the sea breeze, like a vast canopy. On one side was the white sandy road leading into the place. Once up the gracious, curving steps—assisted by doormen who knew just the right welcoming touch—all you could see was the sea.

Sapphire Cove was lovely, and 'Bliss' showed it off at its loveliest.

Abbey refused point blank to use the wheelchair Ryan produced. She hopped up the steps on crutches and gazed in awe out to sea as Ryan booked in. Even Reception wasn't your standard hotel counter. A sleek and beaming lady, immaculately groomed and wonderfully welcoming, tactfully led Ryan to a small cane desk while Abbey and Leith gazed around in awe.

'You wait until I tell my sister I've been here,' Leith breathed. 'One of the kids at school said his brother tried to come here and got kicked out. Oh, Doc Wittner, do you think Dr Henry can afford it?'

'He must be able to,' Abbey said doubtfully. 'I wonder where Janet—'

'They're waiting for us in our villa,' Ryan said, appearing at their elbow like a benevolent genie. He looked down at Abbey's tight face in concern. 'Are you tired? Would you like me to carry you?'

'No. Ryan, we can't... I can't...' Abbey gazed around in consternation. 'Ryan, this place will cost you a mint. I can't possibly pay you back for this.'

'Maybe you already have,' Ryan said gently, and he cupped her chin in his hand and tilted her face, forcing her eyes up to meet his.

'Abbey, we both practise medicine. You choose to practise here for peanuts, and because of you people like me are free to practise elsewhere for sums of money that would probably seem to you to be obscene. Quite simply, that's what I earn, Abbey. It isn't fair but that's the way it is. As a doctor, you've cared for my father for the past four years, and I'm grateful. You work a damned sight harder than I do for a lot less. So shut up now and let me balance the books a little.'

And, without waiting for another protest, he simply swung her up in his arms and headed down the path towards the sea. 'Come on, then, young Leith. Let's see if we can hang ten before lunch.'

They didn't hang ten. Hanging toes over the end of a surfboard here would have meant an immediate bellyflop into the water. Sheltered from open ocean by the Great Barrier Reef, the surf at Sapphire Cove was non-existent.

The water was as calm as a mill pond, but it was far more lovely than any mill pond could ever be. Sparkling blue and stretching on for ever...

The farmer who'd done the milking for Janet had, at Ryan's request, brought Janet and Jack here straight afterwards. Janet met Abbey with a look of wonder. Abbey's mother-in-law was so stunned that she was almost ready to enjoy herself. To Abbey's astonishment, she donned a pair of faded black bathers and was the first to hit the water, whooping with a delight Abbey had never heard from her.

'Ryan says I'm to enjoy myself or he'll take you home,' she told Abbey. She grinned. 'And he says if you go home you're headed for a breakdown. So, with a threat like that hanging over my head, what's a woman to do?' She abandoned her walking stick at the water's edge, forgot her arthritic hip and prepared to follow orders to the letter. She and Jack whooped and splashed in the shallows like two children instead of one staid grandma with grandchild.

And Abbey?

Ryan showed her to their unit, which was right on the water's edge and unbelievably luxurious, allowed her two minutes to change into her bathing costume and then carried her to the shoreline. Here he set her down in the shallows on a cut-away seat—a seat with no legs—and organised another seat for her foot to rest on. His *coup de grâce* was a large green garbage bag which he taped over her massive bandage.

'There. You can't get your bandage wet if you try.'

And then he was off, scooping up the wondering Leith and carrying the little girl out on her first ever serious swimming lesson.

Abbey was left with her mouth open. Stunned as a beached whale.

For a transformation, a genie in a bottle could hardly have done better. She gazed about her in awe. The beach resort was unobtrusively netted, way out. There was no threat of marine stingers here. Janet was lying full length in the shallows, her grandson crowing in delight as he crawled all around her. It was impossible to tell who had the biggest smile, Janet or Jack.

And Leith... The wan little girl was listening seriously to what Ryan was telling her and then putting her face in the water and blowing bubbles. Not such a big deal maybe—but Abbey knew how frightened the little girl was of new experiences and she also knew Leith wasn't accustomed to water.

All of them—Janet, Jack and Leith—were putting their trust absolutely in Ryan Henry. Ryan had told Janet she must drop her isolated grieving and here she was, doing just that. He'd told Leith to leave her terror behind and the child had obeyed.

And what of Abbey?

It was Tuesday morning, for heaven's sake. If anyone had told Abbey the week before that this Tuesday she'd be lying on the beach with her feet up she would have laughed in disbelief. Yet here she was...

She lay back and watched them. Her Jack. Her beloved Janet.

Her Ryan.

The thought brought her up with a jolt.

What had her heart meant by that? It had been an involuntary thought but it stayed, insidious in its appeal.

Her Ryan?

He was no such thing. Once upon a time she'd been proprietorial about Ryan Henry. 'He's *my* friend,' she'd told her mother, and when Ryan had gone off with the big boys to play cricket or football or other boy stuff it had been all Abbey could do not to appear jealous.

Well, he wasn't her Ryan now. He was engaged to be married to a lady called Felicity who, Abbey gathered, could appear at any minute. To claim her own. And Abbey certainly couldn't let her jealousy show then.

Jealousy?

Abbey examined the word from all angles. How could she possibly be jealous of Felicity? After all, she hardly knew Ryan any more. He had left here almost twenty years ago. He was rich and successful and…and practically American.

But she looked out to where Ryan's tanned, muscled body was glistening in the morning sun, the water running in rivulets down his broad back and catching the rays of the sun across the sea. He looked across and laughed at her, his eyes crinkling in just the same way they had when he'd first met her. A long time ago…

Some older girls had been teasing the tiny Abbey on her way to school, and one of them had tipped her lunch out into the dirt. Abbey had sat down, tear-stained and angry, trying to separate the dirt from her sandwiches. Then, all of a sudden, Ryan had been there.

'Kid, I have six whole sandwiches, two chocolate bars and a game of football at lunchtime,' he'd told her. 'I can't possibly manage to eat everything in the time available and if I did I'd get fat. Let's feed your sandwiches to the sea-gulls and divvy up my lunch between us.'

Abbey had looked up through tears at this big, kindly boy with the twinkle and laughter behind his eyes, and her heart had been his ever since.

And, damn, the man just had to look at her now…

'Penny for them.'

Abbey's head jerked up. She'd been playing with a trickle of wet sand as she'd been thinking and hadn't seen Ryan, splashing up through the shallows. Lesson over, Leith had gone to join the fun. Grandma, grandson and now Leith, all pretending to be whales.

'Penny?'

'What are you thinking, Abbey?' Ryan sat himself beside her, and his broad, wet shoulder touched hers. Skin against skin. A shudder of sensation ran though her and Ryan saw it.

'You're cold.'

'No. No, I'm not. How…how did the lesson go?'

'Brilliantly.' He smiled and put his arm around her. A gesture of affection. Nothing more. 'You saw. I have her doing dead man's float already. I had to take things easy because she's exhausted from last night and I don't want a recurrence, but she'll be swimming like a dolphin in no time.'

'Or a whale.' Abbey smiled over to the silly game being played out nearby and tried hard to ignore the sensation of Ryan's arm around her waist.

Ryan grinned. 'As you say.'

'Ryan…' Abbey's voice sounded stiff. 'I want to thank you—'

'There's no need,' Ryan said roughly, and the arm around her waist tightened. Possessively. 'No need at all.'

'But—'

He put his hand up and pressed a finger against her lips. 'Abbey, I said no.' Then he paused.

It was as if he'd suddenly realised how close they were.

And how much was between them.

The glimmers of light that had been dancing all around them suddenly seemed to intensify. Ryan's finger stayed where it was. There was an electric current running between them—running through Ryan's finger on her lips—from Ryan's hand on her waist—from his body straight to hers.

And both of them could feel it. Abbey's eyes flew up to Ryan's and her heart gave a jolt stronger than any gained from a defibrillator.

Ryan…

There was suddenly only Ryan.

Out in the shallows, Janet and the two children were wholly engrossed in their game. Their laughter rang across the water, heightening the sense of delight. Heightening the joy…

And Abbey felt the joy flood through her. Through and through. Ryan holding her. Ryan touching her. It felt so right.

Abbey's face tilted upward to the sun. Lifted compulsively—so her lips were just where Ryan's lips could meet them, if he would only bend his head a little.

And he did.

Ryan stared down at Abbey for a long long moment but he could no more resist the force pulling them together than she could. He couldn't even try.

Ryan's lips met hers as if the two of them were pieces of a puzzle now joined. His chest touched her breast, and her scant bikini bra was no shield at all. Skin against skin. Mouth against mouth. Body against body.

Heart against heart.

That was how it felt, Abbey thought in wonder. As if, by that single touch, Abbey's heart had found a channel to escape—from her body to his. Her lips touched and felt and explored and her whole body yearned to be closer. Closer to this man who made her feel as no man on earth had ever made her feel…

As if she were part of a whole and the other part of her was the man whose lips were claiming hers. And if she drew away she'd be tearing herself in two.

This was crazy. Somewhere in the back of Abbey's head her common sense was screaming at her. Mistake. Huge, earth-shattering mistake. On a scale of one to ten, this ranked about a hundred and forty.

Because the kiss changed everything.

Or, rather, it made everything the same again. It reminded Abbey of what she'd known for most of her life. That she loved Ryan Henry absolutely. Totally. Without question. At eight years old she'd handed her heart over to Ryan and she'd never taken it back again.

Sure, she'd loved John, but her love for John had been different. John had been her beloved friend and he and his mother had been Abbey's family. John and Abbey had built something that was totally satisfying, but there had never been this instant linking of heart to heart, this knowledge that this was where she belonged. That she was part of this man.

Only she didn't belong. She was no part of Ryan Henry.

The kiss was deep and wonderful and lasting, but it couldn't last for ever. A tiny wave splashed up further than the rest, breaking over Ryan's legs, and he drew away as if a bucket of ice water had been thrown at him rather than the tropical warmth of the sea.

As if he was shocked to the core.

'Abbey…'

It was a hoarse whisper, full of total bewilderment, and all Abbey wanted to do was reach out and put her arms around Ryan's broad, wet shoulders and draw him to her again. To claim him as her man.

But she didn't. She couldn't. This man wasn't hers. Ryan's life was half a world away, and the woman he was about to marry was probably on a plane, heading here, right now.

So Abbey gave a choking little laugh and managed to smile.

'That's…that's enough of that, Ryan Henry,' she faltered. 'I know…I know it was only a kiss of friendship but even though this is a honeymoon resort your Felicity would never approve…'

Your Felicity.

The confusion in Ryan's eyes faded. *Felicity.* His future. Felicity was his life. His future had nothing to do with this waif of a doctor, sitting here in her cute little bikini with her elfin-like curls and too-big eyes and her leg stuck out before her, covered with white bandages and a green garbage bag.

Felicity was his love. Not Abbey.

Felicity was his future.

Ryan closed his eyes for a long, long moment and when he opened them his face was resolute.

'You're right. Felicity would have pink kittens. She'd never understand that we're just friends.'

Just friends. How hollow did that sound?

Ryan flicked Abbey's white face with a long finger and rose to stand looking down at her. His eyes were blank and uncomprehending.

'I'd best take Leith back to the hospital,' he told her in a voice that was none too steady. 'I need to check there are no problems with Steve, and then get down to see Dad in the hospital in Cairns tonight.' Ryan bit his lip and stared out to sea, as if reluctant to leave. As he was. Who would want to leave this magic place?

Who would want to leave Abbey?

'I'll be back Thursday if I can,' he told her. 'If Steve's managing, I'll come and see you then. Look after yourself.'

And then, without so much as glancing at Abbey again, he walked over, collected the reluctant Leith and strode away up the beach.

End of one crazy interlude.

Before Ryan left for Cairns he managed to contact Felicity. She was just leaving one meeting and about to enter another.

'I can ring back later,' Ryan told her.

'It's OK, Ryan. There's never going to be a good time here. I'm so busy you wouldn't believe it. What is it?'

Ryan briefly outlined what was happening and heard Felicity frown down the phone line.

'I guess the best course might be for us to just make our own way back to the States,' Ryan suggested. 'I don't want to tie you here. We can do the marriage bit next vacation.'

More frowns. And then a decision.

'No. I'll come anyway,' Felicity said decisively. 'Let's just get this marriage bit over fast, Ryan. It's been hanging over us long enough. I'll be there on Thursday. If you're in Cairns with your father, we can meet there and take it as it comes.'

She rang off and headed for her meeting, leaving Ryan staring down at his mobile phone.

This was what he wanted, wasn't it? That Felicity still came? That the wedding went ahead?

It had to be. It was his future, all mapped out. The future as he and his mother had planned it since he was fifteen years old.

Then why the hell did he feel so damned bleak?

CHAPTER SEVEN

ABBEY'S honeymoon lasted a week, and by the following Monday she was aching for it to be over.

Not that it hadn't been wonderful. Abbey and Janet and Jack had had the time of their lives. Ensconced in absolute luxury, with nothing to do but enjoy themselves, it would have been churlish of them to have done anything else.

Jack had revelled in having his mother and his grandma all to himself. The child had blossomed, steadied on his plump little legs, attacked the water as if he'd been born to it and had chortled and grinned the entire time.

And Janet? The creases on Janet's forehead had faded, and even the look of perpetual pain from her arthritis had eased. She was far fitter now for surgery than she had been a week ago, Abbey thought thankfully.

And Abbey?

Abbey was rested—sort of. It was difficult to sleep, though, lying alone in a king-sized bed with the thought of Ryan Henry's mocking smile staying with her. After the first night Abbey hauled Jack into bed with her, hoping the toddler's faint snoring would ease her sense of loneliness. It didn't. Her sense of isolation stayed.

She should be used to being a widow by now, she told herself fiercely over and over again. There wasn't room in her life for a man.

There was. If that man was Ryan Henry.

But Ryan didn't return. There were a couple of curt phone calls, enquiring as to their welfare, but that had been all.

When Abbey had rung Cairns hospital she'd been told that Sam was 'recovering nicely from his by-pass,' thank you for your enquiry'. When she'd rung Sapphire Cove hospital Eileen had told her Ryan and Steve were coping brilliantly between them and had added, 'Get back to your honeymoon, Abbey Wittner.'

Only it was hard to do that when her heart wasn't really here. It was hard to block out the thought of someone else doing her job. Especially when that someone was Ryan.

And Janet watched her daughter-in-law with troubled eyes and knew why the circles under Abbey's eyes hadn't faded.

She'd seen that kiss…

'You've got everything you need?' Abbey asked, as she stowed Janet's hospital bag in the luggage compartment of the car. 'Though I guess I can always bring in things afterwards. I'll be in and out so often you'll be sick of the sight of me.'

'I've got everything I need except news that the hospital's burned down,' Janet said grimly. 'Why I ever let you and Ryan talk me into this darned fool procedure…'

'Janet, you'll be able to walk again. Pain-free. I promise.'

'Yeah, and next year you'll be at me to have the other hip done.'

'That's right,' Abbey agreed serenely. She and Janet had come back to the farm to pack. Now Abbey handed Jack over to Marcia and pointed to the passenger seat of the car. 'Janet, get in. One of the world's leading orthopaedic surgeons is waiting to perform his artistry on your leg. Let's not keep him waiting.'

'That sounds indecent,' Janet muttered. 'Now if it were you I'd say Ryan Henry could go ahead, no sweat.'

What on earth…? Abbey took a deep breath and fixed her mother-in-law with a defiant look. 'Janet, what do you mean by that?'

'I've got eyes in my head,' Janet said sagely, 'so don't think you can pull the wool over 'em, Abbey Wittner.' She gave Abbey a sideways smile. 'And you've been a widow for close on two years now. Don't you even think about letting the memory of my son get in the way of what's happening between you and that nice young man.'

Abbey licked suddenly dry lips. 'Janet…'

Janet arched her eyebrows. 'Yes?'

'Janet, Ryan Henry is engaged to be married. We haven't heard from him for nearly a week. He might even *be* married by now so you can stop thinking indecent thoughts about the pair of us.'

'Well, if he's married then I'll stop thinking thoughts,' Janet agreed. 'But you're barking up the wrong tree if you think my thoughts are indecent. I happen to be thinking thoughts that are very decent indeed.'

After that, it was hard to get any sort of thought process operating for a while. Abbey eventually pulled up in front of the hospital and there was only one thing in her mind.

She'd see Ryan again.

And he might be married.

Ryan was waiting for them. The car pulled up outside Casualty and Ryan strolled across the car park to greet them. The same Ryan. The same smile. The same twinkle in his eyes. The same impossible charm…

'Janet…' He greeted Abbey's mother-in-law first, and gave her a swift hug. Making himself right at home, Abbey thought bitterly. Making my mother-in-law putty in his hands. 'Glad you decided to trust us.' Then he turned to Abbey. 'You shouldn't be driving.'

'I have full mobility of my foot and it's my left one anyway. My right one's for the brake and that's all that matters.' She said it promptly—so promptly that Ryan laughed.

'You've been rehearsing that line.'

'I knew you'd give me a hard time.'

She did, too. Abbey looked up at Ryan and felt her heart twist. She knew him so well. It was as if the years had peeled away and there was still the same Ryan… Wealthy and respected world-wide, she could still see inside his heart.

'How's Sam?' she said faintly, and blushed. Ryan was looking at her, and if he could read her like she could read him then she was in big trouble. 'How's your father?'

'He's great.' Ryan lifted Janet's bags from the car and took the old lady's arm. 'He said to thank you for the flowers and the chocolates.' He looked at Janet, a faint smile playing at the corner of his mouth. 'Oh, and he said to give you a message, Janet. He says he's had a change of heart so now it's about time you did. Do you think he was talking about your operation—or something else?'

And, to Abbey's astonishment, Janet blushed bright crimson.

'Get away with you,' Janet said fiercely, but she smiled. 'Silly old fool he is. When's he due home?'

'With luck, I'll have him back at the farm by next week.'

'Well…' Abbey stared at her mother-in-law but Janet wasn't meeting her eyes. No questions, her body language said, and Abbey could only acquiesce. Abbey picked up her crutches and the three of them made their way across to the hospital entrance. 'And Felicity?' she asked, still eyeing her mother-in-law.

'She's great, too,' Ryan said curtly.

'Are you married yet?' Janet demanded, and Ryan shook his head.

'Nope. Don't worry. You'll get an invitation. Now, Janet, have you been nil by mouth since midnight?'

'If you mean has Abbey let me eat anything then the answer is not a drop,' Janet said bitterly. 'Not even my breakfast cup of tea. Well, what have you done with this Felicity if you haven't married her?'

Ryan grinned. 'You make it sound like I've stuffed her in a cupboard. You'll meet her soon enough,' Ryan promised, 'but, meanwhile, you and I have a date with a new hip.' He smiled across at Abbey. 'Abbey, Steve's giving the anaesthetic. He's done his first part anaesthetics and is good—but I wondered if you'd like to scrub and assist. Can you manage it, do you think?'

There was nothing Abbey would like better. To sit out in the waiting room—to play the anxious relative instead of doctor—would just about kill her. She gave Ryan her very best smile and nodded.

'Watch you work? I'd love to.'

'Just count the swabs, Abbey girl,' Janet growled. 'I've heard all about surgeons who leave things behind. What goes in has to come out, and I'm depending on you to see to it.'

'Yes, ma'am.'

Ryan's preparations left Abbey stunned.

For a start, Ryan had the theatre as Abbey had never seen it. Designed to cope only with emergency surgery, there was equipment here now that Abbey had had no idea could be begged, borrowed or bought on Sapphire Cove's limited budget.

'It's borrowed,' Ryan said briefly when Abbey queried it. 'Some from Cairns and some from Brisbane.'

'He's pulling in favours all over the place,' Steve told Abbey as they left Ryan, sorting equipment, and went together to don theatre gowns. 'Ryan Henry's one slick operator.'

'Now this I don't understand,' Abbey complained. 'How come Ryan can ask favours in a country he has no contacts in?'

'If you think he has no contacts, how do you think he got me?' Steve demanded. He shoved a theatre cap over his receding hairline and gave her a sheepish smile. 'Favours owed.' Then, at Abbey's look of surprise, he explained.

'Ryan's a world expert in the orthopaedic management of brittle bone disease. He's the best, bar none. And he's generous. Unlike most researchers, he shares his knowledge all over the world. I've been using him as a source for my doctorate in medicine.'

'You're doing a doctorate?'

'Well, at the moment. I spent a bit of time trying to figure out what I wanted to do career-wise. I tried general practice, then anaesthetics and then orthopaedic surgery, but I'm heading more and more for a research-based career. My home base is Cairns but I spent last year in New York, working with Ryan. And Ryan…well, he's been so darned good to me that I can't refuse. That's why I'm here. And there are plenty more like me. He only has to ask.'

He only has to ask…

Abbey tied her gown and scrubbed while she thought this through. It was true enough. More than true. Ryan only had to smile…and then he hardly had to ask at all.

What followed was the slickest piece of surgery that Abbey had ever had the privilege to witness.

Abbey abandoned her crutches—her leg was weight-bearing again anyway—refused Ryan's offer of a stool and stood by to assist in any way she could.

Ryan hardly needed her help. He hardly needed anyone.

This surgery normally took a theatre full of staff. Here there was Eileen, Ryan, Steve and herself, and no one could doubt that Janet was in the best of hands.

From the moment Janet was wheeled into Theatre Ryan concentrated totally on the job in hand, to the exclusion of everything else, and Abbey could only marvel at the speed at which he worked.

He made a swift incision—tiny compared to the incisions Abbey had seen for this procedure before. He dislocated the joint with an ease that left Steve and Abbey exchanging wondering glances. Just as easily, the acetabulum—the cup of the pelvis—was cut away and the prosthetic cup inserted in its place. Then the femur was sliced neatly and the damaged sphere of bone removed. The stem of the prosthesis was wedged skilfully into the shaft of the femur, and the new joint enlocated.

Easy. Fast and simple.

It was just that Ryan made it seem so. It looked easy enough that anyone could do it. Only Steve and Abbey, watching in wonder, knew that the ease Ryan was showing was a skill they could never match with a lifetime of practice.

The last time Abbey had seen this piece of surgery performed it had taken close on three hours. Steve would be able to reverse the anaesthetic in less than one.

Finally Abbey watched as Ryan inserted layers of neat stitching. All Abbey had had to do had been to watch that the tools Ryan needed had been on hand, hold the flaps apart so Ryan could work and supervise as Eileen kept the site free of blood. Now Janet had a new hip and, by the look of Steve's monitors, she'd come through the operation with flying colours.

A new hip... For Janet, that meant almost a new life. She'd been in constant pain for years.

She never would have done it if Ryan hadn't come.

Abbey send a thousand tiny prayers of gratitude upward for this small miracle. She glanced down at her still swollen knee, the bulky dressing barely discernible under her surgical trousers. If it only cost one bruised knee to have Ryan here...well, the bruising was worth it.

How much more would she pay to have him stay? She couldn't begin to consider.

The procedure over, Steve followed his patient out to Recovery. Eileen gathered the stained linen and took herself off to the sluice room, and Abbey was left alone with Ryan.

'Tired?' Ryan asked sympathetically, and immediately Abbey decided she wasn't.

'No.'

'Liar.'

'Well, I shouldn't be tired,' she said. 'Less than an hour for a procedure such as this... I don't know how you did it. Besides, I'm rested and raring to go. There's no excuse for me not to be. I've just pinched your holiday.'

'You needed it. I shouldn't have asked you to assist today.'

'I wanted to,' Abbey said warmly. 'Ryan...' She looked up and met his dark, concerned eyes. 'I just want to thank you,' she said simply. 'If you knew how much I wanted Janet to have this done... The other hip's not nearly as bad but now, even when it finally gives... Well, so far she's come through this brilliantly. As long as her rehabilitation goes well, I shouldn't have any trouble convincing her to do the other hip.'

'I'll fly back and do it for you,' Ryan offered lightly, and Abbey found herself feeling suddenly less bleak.

Maybe when Ryan left here he wouldn't be gone for good. Maybe he would come back in a year or so...

Yeah. In your dreams, Abbey Wittner. Or, if he came back, he'd come back with a wife.

'Where's Felicity?' she said with difficulty, and watched Ryan's face close.

'She's out at my father's farm, working. I asked her to come in for lunch but she hasn't time.'

'I see.' But Abbey didn't. If this was supposed to be a honeymoon, Felicity was surely a trifle offhand about her husband.

'You've not organised the wedding yet?' she asked, and for the life of her she couldn't keep her voice steady.

'No. We'll do that as soon as Dad gets back from Cairns.' It sounded like changing a pair of socks. 'We'll do that.' Just as unimportant.

'Oh.'

This was inane. Abbey crossed to the sink and peeled off her gloves. Then Ryan was behind her, untying the tapes of her theatre garb, and Abbey started feeling really strange.

Really strange.

'You...you can let Steve go back to his research now,' she managed, and it was a real effort to keep her voice light. 'I... You can see my leg's almost back to normal. The lass who's helping to babysit can keep caring for Jack, and I can take over work again.'

'Not yet you can't.'

'Ryan, I must.'

'Monday,' he said. 'You can start again next Monday, but you'll take the rest of the week off, Abbey, and that's an order.'

'No.'

'Yes.'

'Ryan...'

'Don't baulk me here, Abbey,' Ryan said heavily, and his hands suddenly fell to her waist. And gripped hard. 'I want to do this. In three weeks I'm having to walk away from here, and I want to do it with a clear conscience. Allow me to give you a decent break. Then maybe—'

He broke off. His hands fell away and he stepped back as Eileen re-entered the room. Eileen looked curiously from Ryan to Abbey. And she smiled.

'Am I interrupting something?' she said brightly. 'Would you like me to leave clearing this mess until later? And pull the curtains closed?'

Abbey gasped and moved away from Ryan. She hauled her theatre gear from her shoulders and shoved it in the laundry basket with unnecessary force.

'No. No!' The feel of Ryan's hands on her waist was still with her. 'We were just discussing Dr Henry's wedding,' she managed. She took a deep breath. 'If you'll excuse me, R—Dr Henry, I'll go out to Janet. I want to be with her when she wakes.' She took another deep breath. 'And...I accept your offer to work until next Monday, though, if you change your mind...' She faltered, knowing that Eileen's interest was growing by the minute. Probably because of the mounting colour of Abbey's cheeks.

She made a swift, desperate decision.

'If you're free...maybe before Sam comes back...how about on Thursday? Maybe you and Felicity could come to dinner out at the farm. Jack and I would enjoy having you.'

There. She'd got it out. She had to start treating this man as part of a couple, she thought bleakly, and the best way to do it was to put a face to this mysterious Felicity. The sooner the better.

'You mean it?' Ryan asked, and Abbey nodded.

'Thursday. Seven o'clock?' She cast a rather frantic look at Eileen. 'Can you come too?'

'I'm on duty,' Eileen said sadly, but there was a hint of a twinkle behind her eyes. 'Otherwise I wouldn't miss it for quids. I'm just not sure where Felicity stands in all this.

I'm just not sure where anyone does. But I'd really like to know.'

'Why am I doing this?'

Abbey stared down at her tousle-headed toddler and demanded an answer. 'Jack, why am I going to all this trouble? It's like those people who go swimming in the Antarctic in midwinter. I'd have to be a little bit crazy.'

Jack was armed with a spoon and was in the process of cleaning the chocolate mousse bowl. There was chocolate mousse from one end of his small person to the other and he had far more important matters weighing on his mind than his mother's social life. Like how he could get the last scraps of chocolate right at the bottom of the bowl...

He gave up and did it the easy way. Abandoning the spoon, he stuck his head right down the bottom of the bowl and licked.

And Abbey chuckled.

'Yeah, well, the ostrich approach may have its advantages, but they're coming even if I stick my head in a mixing bowl too.' She sighed and looked around her. At least the food would be great. If there was one thing Abbey could do well it was cook. If only the house didn't look so...so...well, so darned poor.

It normally didn't matter. It was just that tonight...tonight what she really didn't want to happen was for Felicity and Ryan to feel sorry for her.

'Which they shouldn't,' she said. She picked up Jack, bowl and all, and gave his chocolate-clad person a fierce hug. It was a bit tricky as he still had the bowl over his head, but Jack enjoyed the sensation and gave a chuckle from the bottom of the bowl. 'I have you, Jack Wittner. And I have Janet. Your grandma is improving every day, little Jack, and we'll have her playing hopscotch in no time.'

Felicity and Ryan arrived right on seven and by the time they arrived Abbey had the place looking as good as it ever could. She'd placed a white cloth (not too worn) over the scrubbed kitchen table and a bunch of crimson bougainvillea sprayed from a glass jar in the centre. With luck the flowers were so lovely that her visitors would miss the absence of a cut crystal vase. The meal was all ready. The smell from the chicken concasse was wonderful and Abbey was almost satisfied.

She gave herself one last critical look in the mirror before she went to answer the door. Maybe her soft white frock was a little worn but it was still pretty, with a low scooped neckline, no sleeves and a skirt that flared out into soft folds almost to her ankles. Abbey's close-cropped curls were brushed until they shone and she'd even scrounged a little make-up from a store she hadn't used since John died.

'Your mummy looks pretty,' she told Jack in a voice that sounded defiant. Jack was dressed in his newest pyjamas and was clearly not impressed. He had a new game. The chocolate bowl was now clean, but Jack had it permanently over his head. He staggered about like a flannelette and plastic robot, bumping into everything in sight and chuckling with glee. Now he hauled his bowl off his head, checked out the new version of his mother—and stuck his bowl back.

Abbey stuck her tongue out at her now blind son.

'As a first comment, I'd have to say your appraisal stinks,' she told her son, but she smiled and went to answer the door, feeling good.

That lasted a whole ten seconds. Abbey swung open the door and her feeling of satisfaction in her person, her little house and the evening in general faded to nothing.

Felicity was just gorgeous.

Of course she was. She was Ryan's intended wife, after all, and Abbey might have known Ryan could never marry anyone second rate.

Felicity was tall—almost as tall as Ryan—and willow-slim, with legs that seemed to go on for ever. Her dress must have cost a bomb and it was straight out of the New York collections. Elegant and understated, it was high at the neck and minimal everywhere else, sleekly black and hugging Felicity's body as if it had been sewn on her. Felicity's long blonde hair hung down freely, beautifully cut and silken smooth. Luminous blue eyes gazed at Abbey with lazy interest, and her perfectly painted mouth curved into a smile of greeting.

It was all Abbey could do not to slam the door shut again.

But Ryan was beside Felicity, looking so handsome he almost took Abbey's breath away. His dark suit looked as expensive as Felicity's gown, but the smile behind his eyes was infinitely warmer than Felicity's. He smiled straight down at her and Abbey felt her heart turn to butter.

'Boo,' said Jack. He appeared from behind his mother's skirts, lifted his bowl—and then saw the newcomers. Stunned by the power of his boo, he scuttled off toward the kitchen, his bowl back in place. He made it as far as the first wall, thumped against it hard, toppled over and started to wail.

After that, the evening went straight downhill.

The meal itself was fine.

Abbey's cooking couldn't be faulted. With Jack tucked safely in bed—still clutching his bowl ready for robotics in the morning—Abbey served and tried to take part in a conversation in which she felt increasingly uneasy. Felicity ate as if she hardly noticed what she was eating, making no comment on the trouble Abbey had gone to. She chatted brightly, with an air Abbey knew from long ago. Ryan's mother had it down to an art form.

It was the air of a social superior putting the lower orders at their ease.

'This house is charming, Abbey,' Felicity said pleasantly. 'It's just so quaint. Almost an artwork in itself. If I could lift it up and take it back to New York it'd sell for a fortune.'

'With or without the rising damp?' Abbey managed a smile and then tried to at least make the conversation medical. When in doubt, work. 'Ryan tells me you're an oncologist. While you're here I wonder if I could have a talk to you about one or two cancer patients and their treatment. I'd very much appreciate it.'

She would, too. It was hard sometimes to be an isolated family doctor, suspecting that the treatment she was giving was less than optimal but not sure. With simply no time to attend conferences and keep up to date, Abbey called for specialist advice often, but sometimes her patients refused to go to Cairns to see someone better qualified. If she had someone on the spot…a well-trained oncologist…she'd love to know what the latest treatments were.

But Felicity was holding her hands up in horror.

'I'm in research,' she said firmly. 'I don't see actual patients any more. Ryan and I are heading for what we think of as ideal medical practices. Ones where we don't handle grubby patients at all.'

'Oh. Of course.' Abbey cleared the dinner plates and counted to ten. Then she tried again. 'Actually, I'd only like to talk to you about treatments. I am a bit out of touch here, and it'd be lovely if you could give me an hour or so of your time—just to answer a few questions that have been troubling me.'

'That's what journals are for,' Felicity said lightly. 'I think you've taken up enough of my honeymoon, don't you, dear?'

It was the 'dear' that got her.

Abbey turned to find Ryan glowering, and she couldn't figure out whether he was glowering at her for asking the question or glowering at Felicity for rebuffing her so well.

It didn't matter. Ryan Henry was engaged to the cow and he was responsible. Abbey glowered right back at him. She glowered at the pair of them. She glowered at the kitchen in general.

'There's chocolate mousse,' she said tightly, and dumped it on the table with a slap that would, if she'd been waitressing at the Ritz, have got her the sack before she could have blinked. Which was just what she wanted. She wanted to be dismissed. She felt young and country-bumpkin frumpish and she even wanted Ryan to go home. Just get them both out of here.

She ate one spoonful of chocolate mousse—funny that Jack liked it because as far as Abbey could tell it tasted like mud—and then the phone rang.

Thank heaven for phones. Only this time the thought was inappropriate.

Abbey lifted the receiver and it was Marg Miller.

'*Abbey...Abbey...*'

Chocolate mousse, Felicity—even Ryan—forgotten, Marg Miller suddenly had Abbey's full attention. There was no mistaking the terror flooding down the line.

'Marg, what is it? No! Marg, you need to stop crying. Take your time. Three deep breaths and then say what's wrong.'

Abbey waited while the ragged breathing steadied. When Marg spoke again, at least Abbey could understand her.

'Abbey, it's Ian. He came home last night. From Sydney. Abbey, he looks just awful...'

'He's ill?'

'Yes, but... Not ill... I mean... Abbey, he's gone...'

'Is he dead?'

The shock tactic worked. Marg gave a terrified gasp and then steadied. When she spoke again her voice was almost calm.

'Abbey, I just don't know.'

'Is he there with you?' Abbey had visions of a heart attack now. Ian dead on Marg's kitchen floor. She cast an urgent glance at Ryan, who was rising to his feet. She had Ryan's total attention, as Marg Miller had hers.

'No. He's not. Abbey, that's just it. I don't know...'

'Marg, what is it that you're afraid of?' Abbey demanded harshly, making her voice as authoritative as she could. 'Quickly. Just say. I can't help unless you do.'

Silence.

And then Marg's voice, breaking with sobs again.

'Abbey, he came home just miserable. He'd hardly speak to me. Just went to bed and stayed there. Today he went out for a walk. He walked for ages and when he came home he seemed…well, odd. But he wouldn't say what was wrong. Then tonight…I had to go out to a CWA dinner and Ian said just go. He said I mustn't stay home because of him.

'So I went but when I got there I started thinking—you know when you think there's something really, awfully wrong but you don't know what? And I came home. But he's not here. Abbey, there's a note on my bed, saying goodbye. And he's sorry. And…and his car's gone and… Abbey, I know this is stupid but so is the hose I keep by the kitchen door. Abbey, he wouldn't… You don't think…? He wouldn't—'

'What's he driving?' Abbey snapped.

'A red Corolla.'

'Licence number?'

'Abbey, I don't know.' Marg's voice broke into a wail and Abbey clipped it off fast.

'OK, Marg. Ring your sister. Tell her to come over and be with you.' Marg's sister lived on the adjoining property, Abbey thought thankfully, and Annette was a sensible woman who could be relied on in an emergency. 'I'll contact the police to get things mobilised, and I'll be right there.'

'You don't think… Abbey, if I'm being stupid…'

'Marg, do you believe Ian intends suicide?'

There was a sharp, horrible pause.

'Yes, I do,' Marg said bleakly. 'I don't know why but, God help us, Abbey, yes, I do. Please, Abbey, hurry.'

'I'm coming.'

CHAPTER EIGHT

RYAN came with her.

It took three minutes before they were in Abbey's car, heading for the Miller property, and by then Abbey felt like all the wind had been pushed right out of her. If there was one thing Ryan Henry could do, it was mobilise help in an emergency.

He organised Jack while Abbey contacted the police. By the time Abbey was off the phone she knew there was no way Felicity would look after Jack. Abbey would never have thought of asking it of her but Ryan knew no qualms. He asked but he got nowhere. Felicity took herself off in Ryan's car, clearly appalled that Ryan felt the need to get involved. Abbey heard her talking angrily while she was waiting for the police sergeant to answer his mobile phone.

'For heaven's sake, Ryan, this is none of your business. These people have nothing to do with you.'

Ryan didn't respond to Felicity's anger at all. 'I'll see you later, Felicity,' Ryan said flatly. 'I'll go over the road and find the girl who looks after Jack...'

Their voices faded out of range and Abbey blocked Felicity's anger out of her mind. She simply didn't have time to think about it.

She rang the ambulance as well as the police, asking the officers to take the vehicle out to the Millers'.

'I hope I'm overreacting here,' she said to herself. 'I hope Marg's overreacting.'

But Marg Miller was a sensible, unemotional woman who'd buried a husband and raised a family of six on her own, and Abbey had never known her to panic before.

With a sinking heart, Abbey slipped off her dress, hauled on jeans and a sweatshirt and emerged to find Marcia had already arrived from over the road. Ryan was a mover and

113

shaker if anyone was. The next thing Abbey knew they were turning out of the driveway, with Ryan at the wheel of her car.

'Tell me where to go, Abbey,' Ryan said curtly.

'Just straight north.' She paused. 'You know the Miller farm?'

'I think so. Off Palm Road.'

'That's the one.' Abbey frowned. 'It's not much use us going there, though. Ryan, where would you go if you took off in your car from the Millers' with a piece of rubber hose, and suicide in mind? You'd need a spot where no one would find you until morning.'

'Mmm.'

There was silence while the little car cut through the night. Outside was still and warm and starlit. It was a lovely night. Hardly a night for ending your life.

'Ryan...when I asked for your help with Mrs Miller and told you I thought there was something wrong with Ian...did you contact him?' Abbey said diffidently into the darkness. She tried as hard as she could to make her voice non-judgemental but it still came out badly. And Ryan heard it.

'No.'

'Oh.'

Silence.

'Hell,' Ryan said at last. 'I didn't see the need. It was none of my business. I rang his mother like you asked.'

'And?'

'And she said she was worried about Ian's health. So I told her to have him make an appointment with you or Steve or me next time he was home. Or see his own doctor in Sydney.'

'Just like he would if he had a sore throat,' Abbey said softly.

'How the hell was I to know he was suicidal?'

'You weren't to know that,' Abbey agreed. 'I should have rung myself.'

'Abbey, Ian's health is none of our business.'

'No. Like Felicity said...'

'Abbey...'

'Just shut up, Ryan,' Abbey said, in a voice that dragged. 'You've changed from the Ryan I knew and loved. I don't think I know you any more, but I guess it doesn't matter. It's not us that's important here. Just...just think about where Ian would go.'

'Thomlinsons'.'

Ryan's voice three minutes later, cutting across the silence, made Abbey jump. Her mind had been racing in a million directions, and she didn't like where she ended up each time. How long had Ian been away? Marg hadn't known. How long had he had to carry out what he intended?

'Pardon?'

'Thomlinsons',' Ryan said heavily. 'You must know the place, Abbey. The cove where we swam out to rescue old man Thomlimson's crayfish?'

Abbey frowned. And considered.

The Thomlinsons ran a derelict property just north of the Millers'. The ground on the Thomlinsons' place was rough and hilly, giving way to mountains behind. From the foot of the mountains the land turned into uncultivated wilderness.

Going north from the Millers' the road turned to gravel. Just before the Thomlinsons' farmhouse there was a track, leading off to a tiny cove nestled deep in the hills. Very few people knew about it. Ryan and Abbey had found it on their bikes as kids, and then they'd seen old man Thomlinson collecting his crays so they'd gone back time and time again to rescue his catch.

'Ian would know about it,' Abbey said slowly. 'He was brought up on the Miller place, and all the Miller kids knew every inch of the coastline around here. Almost as well as we did.'

'Ian would know the cove is deserted. There's room down there to turn a car but that's all. And he could sit and look out to sea until...' He didn't go on.

'Let's try there,' Abbey said decisively. She motioned to the mobile phone on her belt. 'We're not too far away that we can't get back in a hurry if he's found elsewhere, but... Oh, Ryan, may you please be right.'

He was.

Two minutes later Ryan nosed the little car gently off the road and onto the track leading down to the beach. They bumped over three or four sandhills and came to a halt.

There was a car in front of them, facing out towards the sea, and in the moonlight they could see the car had a hosepipe leading from the exhaust up to the driver's window.

Dear heaven...

Ryan was out of the car almost before it stopped. Even hindered by her weak knee, Abbey wasn't far behind, but by the time she reached him Ryan had the driver's door open and was dragging the unconscious Ian out of the car.

The stench of exhaust fumes was almost overwhelming. Abbey shoved her hand up to her mouth, coughed and gagged but kept on coming.

'No.' Ryan's voice was clipped and curt, stopping her in her tracks. He kept moving, dragging Ian's body clear of the car and onto the green verge of seagrass. Away from the fumes.

'Get your bag, Abbey,' he ordered swiftly. 'Fast. Move! I think he's still alive.'

What followed were several frantic minutes.

By the time Abbey reached him with her bag Ryan had already cleared the airway. Abbey found the mask, positioned the oral airway into Ian's mouth and started breathing for him. Ryan started cardio-pulmonary resuscitation. They worked together as a team, each concentrating fiercely on what they had to do.

And three minutes later they had their reward. Ian's body heaved, he retched into the mask and then, as Abbey moved to clear his airway, he retched again and his lungs heaved for air.

Had they been in time?

No longer needed for breathing, Abbey helped Ryan swing Ian onto his side to prevent him choking. It was only three or four minutes since they'd arrived. Not very long, but how long hadn't Ian been breathing before they'd got to him?

It couldn't have been that long if CPR worked so quickly, Abbey told herself, but maybe that was wishful thinking.

Ian's eyelids flickered open. His eyes moved uncertainly from Abbey to Ryan in the soft moonlight and he groaned.

'No!'

'Ian…'

'Damn you. No. Put me back. Put me back…'

Well, that was a start. Ryan gave Abbey a half-hearted grin, felt for Ian's pulse and his grin broadened.

Ian was definitely going to live.

One problem was over, but this was only the first step, Abbey knew. How many would-be suicides had been rescued or revived, only to suicide successfully later? Heaven knew, but the list must be legion.

At least Ian had a chance now. Abbey could try to communicate, even if Ryan hadn't.

Even if Ryan thought it was none of her business.

'It's OK, Ian.' Abbey's arm went around Ian's shoulder and she hugged him in a gesture that had nothing to do with being a doctor but everything to do with the fact that she'd known Ian since childhood and his mum was her friend. 'We're here for you. I don't know what the problem is that's so awful you had to take this step but, whatever it is, we're with you and we'll be here tomorrow for you. Just relax now. Concentrate on getting your strength back. We'll take you to hospital and talk through your hassles in the morning.'

'No.' It was a fierce, fretful whisper. 'Don't touch me. Don't… Leave me alone. You can catch…'

But Ryan was bending over, and he suddenly took Ian's hand and gripped hard.

'Ian, have you got AIDS?' he demanded flatly.

Ian's eyes widened. He stared from Ryan to Abbey and then back to Ryan. And his face closed in misery.

'Oh, God…'

'Is that why you did this?'

'What do you think?' Ian whispered. 'HIV positive… Oh, God…'

'Hey, Ian, AIDS isn't the end of the world,' Ryan said strongly. 'It's not even a death sentence. I've just come from New York and the latest breakthroughs are amazing.' His grip tightened. Ian was firmly held by the pair of them.

This was no clinical approach. This was two humans comforting another in any way they could, and Abbey could only wonder at the concern in Ryan's voice. She hadn't thought him capable of such concern for someone he hardly knew.

This was the old Ryan, then. Not Felicity's Ryan.

'Ian, let me talk to you about this in the morning,' Ryan said. 'But for now…rest and know that when you wake up you won't be by yourself. Abbey and I are here to help. Your mum's worried sick and the old prejudices about your illness are disappearing fast. I promise you, what's in front of you isn't worth dying over now. I promise you, mate.'

And he stayed with his hand gripping Ian's until the ambulance arrived. Then Ian closed his eyes with exhaustion and let the medical world do its will with him.

'How did you guess he has AIDS?'

'Intelligence,' Ryan said promptly—so promptly that Abbey burst out laughing. They were back in the car again, travelling south. Steve had been telephoned and was waiting for Ian at the hospital. Mrs Miller would be there too. There was no urgency for their return, and the night seemed suddenly light and free and lovely.

Tragedy averted.

'So, tell me how your mighty intelligence worked it out?' Abbey demanded, and Ryan grinned.

'How about intuition?'

'That's worse.'

'It's partly what it was, though,' Ryan told her. 'I knew Ian at school—remember? I remember him being a loner, and thinking maybe he was gay. That's not enough on its own, and he was still a teenager, but the look of him…the fear…the worry that you might be infected if you touched him… At a guess, he's HIV positive, he's working on out-of-date information and he's terrified.'

'I see.'

Abbey nodded, thinking it through. It made sense. Ian had done law at Sydney university and very rarely came home. All the other Miller kids were married and settled by now, but Abbey had never heard any hint of a romantic attachment for Ian.

Oh, dear. This was some end to her dinner party. At least, though, they'd been in time.

'I think you mean trouble, Ryan Henry,' Abbey said as they turned out of the cove. 'Things have gone haywire since you arrived. To use CPR twice in ten days… Believe it or not, it's been six months since I've tried to resuscitate anyone, and then I failed. It hardly seems fair that you've done it twice successfully in this short a time. You'll be thinking I go from one drama to another.'

'Don't you?' Ryan demanded wryly, and Abbey shook her head.

'Nope. But…as you can see, when I'm needed I'm really needed,' she added thoughtfully. 'That's why I'll never leave here. If I left… Well, if Sapphire Cove had doctors at all it'd be overseas doctors who think a tropical resort sounds wonderful. I've seen them come and go from other places around here. They stay through our winter and think it's magic and then comes summer and they can't wait to leave! February here tries anyone's temper.'

'I remember summer in Sapphire Cove,' Ryan said, thinking back to a time it had been so hot even shorts and thongs had seemed too much trouble to wear. 'Though I have to say I kind of like summer here. All the rain and frogs and insects—and the odd cyclone thrown in for good measure.' He hesitated. 'At least it must get quieter for you. When the wet hits your population must fall.'

'Mmm, but the ones that stay get sicker,' Abbey told him. 'I get so many tropical infections. The water gets warmer, with particles of coral floating everywhere. People go swimming with a tiny scratch and it turns into a major infected wound.' She sighed. 'Well, that's my business. You'll be long gone by February.'

Then she hesitated. She needed Ryan's help before he left. 'You will have a really long talk to Ian tomorrow, though, won't you, Ryan? I don't know the up-to-date treatments for AIDS. In fact, I've never treated an AIDS patient. I can't reassure him as he needs to be reassured.'

'I'll phone a friend in New York tonight for information,' Ryan agreed. 'He's working in the field and he has the disease himself. If anyone can give me the latest, Marcus can. And then I'll talk to Ian in the morning.'

Abbey bit her lip. 'You…you promise?'

Silence.

'You really do think I've changed, don't you, Abbey?' Ryan said softly, but his knuckles on the steering-wheel were white. 'Hell, Abbey, I said I would.'

'I'm sorry. It's just…well, it's Ian's life. And…and I'm already blaming myself for tonight. If I hadn't depended on you—'

'Yeah.' Ryan's voice was curt and angry. 'Let's all blame Ryan.' He cast a swift glance at her. 'Why not? I do myself.' He shrugged. 'And I'm sorry. Believe me, Abbey, you can't blame me any more than I do myself.

'I guess—doing what I do—well, my job's mostly research and teaching, and when I am called in for hands-on work the patient's been counselled and assessed already. Often they're already unconscious on the operating table. You get used to thinking of problems as a pelvis or a femur or a combination of problems—not as Mr Jones whose life depends on what you're doing.'

He sighed. 'I guess I hadn't realised until tonight—or maybe I once knew but had forgotten—that what I do has a wider impact. It certainly did tonight—or, rather, what I didn't do. It damn near caused a tragedy.'

He stared straight ahead again and kept on driving, and Abbey bit her lip as she watched his drawn face. She should have shut up. Ryan hadn't changed so much that she had to kick him when he was already feeling so guilty.

She turned away and glanced out of the car. They were travelling along the beach road towards the town, and the moon was glimmering over the sea in a brilliant band of gold. The beach stretched away on either side—a broad ribbon of sand, smooth and washed clean in the moonlight. It was low tide and Sapphire Cove was at its most beautiful. Not a tourist in sight. Nothing.

Except...

'Ryan, stop!'

Abbey's voice was urgent, and Ryan acted instinctively. He shoved his foot on the brake so hard that if they hadn't been wearing seat belts both would have been catapulted through the windscreen.

'What on earth...?'

'Pull over, Ryan.' Abbey's voice was excited rather than fearful. She was staring down at the beach in wonder. 'Oh, Ryan...'

And Ryan looked. And saw...

A vast turtle was lumbering up the beach, causing a swathe in the wet sand like a bulldozer ploughing a channel. The turtle was heading in a straight line up the beach, and that could only mean one thing. As far as Ryan knew, turtles came out of the sea for one purpose. To lay eggs.

'Oh, Ryan...' Abbey was scarcely breathing. 'After all this time...'

She hauled open the car door and was out, heading across the sandy verge to the beach beyond. Like it or not, Ryan was left to follow.

Abbey and Ryan watched the turtle for almost two hours, and they hardly spoke for the entire time.

What they were seeing was a miracle. The huge green

turtles were increasingly rare in these waters. They came up onto the beach to lay their eggs, but there were thousands of miles of coastline for them to choose and for one to choose this place...and this time...

All Abbey's life she had wanted to see one lay her eggs. And, back in the time when he'd been her friend, so had Ryan. So Abbey assumed he was as spellbound as she. As eager to see.

And, miraculously, for once in her busy life Abbey could take the time to watch. Abbey had a babysitter who wasn't expecting them home soon. Steve was in charge at the hospital. For once in her life Abbey was free.

She crouched low in the seagrass and was silent as the big turtle lumbered up almost within touching distance and started to dig.

The turtle was almost two feet wide and three feet long—massive—and nothing was getting in her way. Whether or not she was aware of Ryan and Abbey's presence, she kept on digging, but Abbey wouldn't have distracted her for the world. She didn't have to warn Ryan to stay still or be silent. Ryan sank on the sand beside her and watched by her side.

And watched.

And watched.

And, in a way, this time was a healing for them both. For Abbey the last years had moved like a fast-paced nightmare. John's death. The birth of Jack. Financial disaster and the constant pressures of far too much work.

And Ryan?

Ryan watched the turtle, preparing a safe place for her brood, and he felt his foundations shift. Or what he'd thought of as his foundations.

He hadn't known until this moment that he'd left a part of him here when he'd left this place. At fifteen his mother had dragged him half a world away and had set about systematically destroying every memory he'd had of his childhood. His father hadn't really cared, she'd said. Why else hadn't he fought her for custody? Sapphire Cove had nothing except a bunch of country hicks and no culture at all.

Close on twenty years of her poisoned tongue had had their effect. He'd almost started believing her.

But now in this time of absolute stillness and wonder—crouching side by side with Abbey in the sand—their bodies touching and yet not speaking at all—letting the moonlight play on their faces as it lit up the wonder of new life before them—Ryan knew that his mother was wrong.

Sure, in New York he had a life that his mother was proud of. But was it his life?

He sat and he watched and he thought. Two hours was nothing—and yet two hours had the power to change people's lives.

They stayed where they were as a miracle happened before their eyes. The moonlight cast a soft glow over the whole beach, lighting the scene almost like day.

The turtle knew exactly what she was doing. She scraped a vast hole behind her, using her paddles to shove the sand aside. Occasionally a spray of fine sand flew up over Abbey and Ryan and it was as much as Abbey could do not to laugh in delight.

And then came the eggs…

Slowly they came, one after another. Eggs, eggs and more eggs. Soft white balls, plopping moistly into their bed of sand. A huge mound of new life, just waiting to happen.

And finally the last egg was laid and the turtle's job was almost complete. Once more those massive paddles shifted the sand, but this time they calmly coated her eggs—slowly, carefully—leaving no egg uncovered. And then, magically, as though receiving final acclaim for a job well done, the great turtle turned and looked straight at Ryan and Abbey.

Straight in the eye. Eyeball to eyeball. As if challenging them to keep her eggs safe.

And then she calmly turned towards the ocean and made her way majestically back to sea. The waves washed over her as she reached the shallows, the sea took her back into its warmth and all there was left to tell them she'd really been here was a tract of furrowed sand leading down to the sea. And Abbey and Ryan were left staring after her in wonder.

'She knew,' Abbey breathed. 'Did you see? She knew we were here all the time. She let us watch.'

'Yeah, well, she must have known we were doctors.' Ryan smiled but he felt a bit emotional all the same. In truth, he felt very emotional.

It was all too much. This place. This woman. His friend…

It was bringing his childhood back again fast. How many October and November nights had he and Abbey hunted along this beach, searching for just what they had seen tonight? They'd never found a breeding turtle, but they'd always been sure they would.

'Just one more night,' Abbey had pleaded over and over again when Ryan had tried palming her off with homework commitments or somesuch. But the breeding season was short and Ryan had never tried hard to think of reasons he shouldn't come. He'd longed to find one as much as Abbey had. They'd crept out when their respective mothers had thought they'd been long in bed, and if Abbey's mother had suspected the reason her daughter wore dark shadows under her eyes for most of the turtle-breeding months she'd never let on she knew.

And then Ryan had gone.

'But we've never even found a turtle yet,' Abbey had wailed when Ryan had told her he was going.

She'd put the pain aside with her heartache for Ryan, and she'd stopped searching. Somehow it hadn't seemed important to find a turtle when Ryan hadn't been here to share it with her.

But now Ryan was back—and they'd found their turtle.

Abbey turned to face him, and found him watching her, and the wonder in her heart was reflected in his eyes.

'Abbey…'

'Did you ever see anything so beautiful?' she breathed, and Ryan's hands came out to take hers.

'No, Abbey, I never have.'

And suddenly he wasn't talking about the turtle.

And Abbey wasn't thinking about the turtle.

There was only the linking of their hands.

There was only what was between them.

Ryan.

Her friend.

Her love.

And then there was nothing between them any more. Nothing. Not even distance. Somehow the length of their arms which had been there was gone. Somehow Ryan's head was bending and Abbey's was tilting upwards to meet him. To welcome him. To taste him and to know this man who was a part of her already. Whom she already knew in every way but this.

And then his lips were claiming hers and Abbey's mouth was opening beneath his to acknowledge his claim. This was so right. So...so meant. Like the turtle they'd been looking for since childhood and had finally found. They'd known they would find her. And maybe...maybe Abbey had always known this was her place. Here was her home. Ryan's arms were where she was meant to be. Like the turtle, this was a miracle searched for and found.

Ryan...

Ryan's hands were falling to her waist. Somehow they were no longer sitting, but settling deeper into their sandy hollow so their bodies were cocooned against each other. The sand, warm from the heat of a day of tropical sun, welcomed and embraced them. Above them were the moon and the stars and the night sky. And holding them all together was her Ryan.

Ryan...

Abbey returned his kiss, gently at first but then with increasing fierceness—possessiveness. Ryan was hers. Hers! What right had he had to go away and leave her all those years ago? What right had he to marry Felicity?

The thought of Felicity flashed into Abbey's mind but she shoved it away as her hands wound themselves around Ryan's broad shoulders and her breasts pushed against his chest. Dear God, she wanted him. Ryan…

Felicity.

The thought flashed back again. Abbey shoved it away with everything she possessed—but the thought wouldn't go.

It wouldn't.

Felicity.

And Ryan felt it.

Wondering, Ryan drew back a little in the moonlight.

'Abbey?' he said, and his voice was a husky murmur, laced with desire. 'Love?'

'Felicity,' she said flatly.

Silence.

Abbey pushed Ryan back and rolled sideways in the sand. She stood, uncertain, refusing to look at Ryan. Refusing to look at her love.

'T-take me home, Ryan,' she said softly. 'I think…we must both have been mad. You're engaged to Felicity, re-member?'

Deny it, her heart was screaming, but Ryan didn't. Instead, he stood and looked gravely down at her. When he spoke again his voice was harsh and bleak.

'As you say. We've both run mad. Gone troppo has meaning after all.'

And that was that. End of evening.

'Help me hide the turtle tracks before we go,' Abbey managed, staring out to sea. Concentrating on anything but the pain in her heart.

There was something else to concentrate on. The eggs *must* be protected. There were all sorts of predators who'd see the turtle's furrow before the tide came back in. The best disguise was simply to make more furrows—so it looked like the sand had been disturbed by a party of re-vellers rather than one solitary turtle. And put plenty of human scents around to deflect interest.

Ryan nodded. Like Abbey, he was searching for something to say. Something to do that didn't touch the jumble of his emotions. He left Abbey and retrieved a huge piece of dried seaweed. Silently he started raking it back and forth across the sand.

For a long moment Abbey watched him, and then silently started to do the same.

There were shadows haunting Ryan, she thought bleakly, and one of those shadows was her. She could feel Ryan's desire. But she knew... Well, Abbey knew his mother and she knew Felicity. She knew what she was up against.

Finally they finished and made their way back to the car.

'There are a group of turtle-watchers in town,' Abbey managed as they settled back in the car for the drive home.

Her voice was flat and desolate. She was no longer excited about the turtle. She just wanted to get home. Get to the sanctuary of her pillows so she could hide her head and have a good howl. 'I'll let them know where the eggs are. They'll work out the gestation period and set up a watch when they're due.'

If they could, the turtle-watchers would try to be here when the eggs hatched. The journey from the nest to the sea was the most hazardous the turtles would face. Often almost all the tiny hatchlings were eaten by gulls and other predators before they reached the water.

'I'd love to be here when they hatch,' Abbey added.

Silence.

'If I can I'll send you a photograph,' Abbey offered, and Ryan's gut clenched into an almost unbearable ache.

She'd send him a photograph to put on the wall in his office. So he could remember this night always.

He couldn't bear it.

Felicity was on the telephone when Ryan arrived back at his father's farm. She greeted him with a cool smile, a lift of her eyebrows and a wave to the coffee-pot.

Ryan obliged. He made her coffee and then sat and waited for his love to finish speaking to New York.

His love?

His future.

He should be working, too, he told himself. He was running so far behind. And tonight...tonight he'd spent the whole night watching a turtle. What a waste!

Yeah?

If he told her, Felicity would agree it was a waste. His colleagues back in New York would think it was a waste.

Or maybe they wouldn't. Maybe they'd be as jealous as hell.

'What's the time in New York?' he asked when Felicity finally finished her phone call. She was typing furiously into her lap-top computer and clearly had no time for small talk.

'About eleven mid-morning. What kept you? Did you find your suicide, then?' It was only half a question. When Felicity worked she committed herself absolutely. It was one of the things Ryan admired about her. She had a brilliant mind, a brilliant body and...

And?

He gave himself a mental shake. What the hell was he thinking of? There was no 'and'. Felicity was everything he needed in a woman.

Everything he wanted?

'We found him,' he said grimly. 'He has AIDS.'

Felicity frowned. 'Was the suicide successful?'

'No. Close, but we found him in time. We resuscitated him.'

'Ryan!' Suddenly he had all Felicity's attention. She stared up at him, appalled. 'Ryan, I hope you took precautions.'

'We used a mask.'

'And gloves? Ryan, for heaven's sake, resuscitating AIDS patients is not your job. If that's what Abbey wants to do, fine, but to haul you in... She has no right.'

No. She didn't. Abbey had no right to ask anything of him at all.

And the thought of her not having that right made Ryan sick at heart.

Abbey was his friend.

With a huge mental shake Ryan managed to shove the thought of Abbey aside—the thought of Abbey in his arms—yielding her slim body to his. Clinging to him. Welcoming his kiss as if it was right.

She was lovely, but Abbey wasn't his future. She couldn't be. Abbey was a widow and a mother and she had obligations up to her neck. Someone like Abbey would fit into his New York life like a fish out of water.

He shrugged—and turned to phone New York.

Turned to get on with his life.

CHAPTER NINE

AT EIGHT the next morning there were three doctors in Sapphire Cove hospital, and Sister Eileen Roderick was enjoying herself.

'I'm sorry, Doctors, but I don't have enough nursing staff to accompany each of you on ward rounds,' she said primly. 'I can offer one of you Ted, but otherwise you'll have to share.'

'How about if Dr Wittner goes back on honeymoon where she's supposed to be?' Ryan said darkly, glowering at Abbey. Abbey was dressed in a soft blue dress that exactly matched her eyes, her curls were bouncing and shining and she looked altogether too pretty for words.

'How about if Dr Henry goes back to New York?' Abbey retorted, flushing. Ryan Henry looked too darned handsome for his own good. Or for her peace of mind. And how on earth could she concentrate on anything other than the memory of that kiss?

'Well, I'm not going back to Cairns,' Steve interjected. 'This place is too much fun.'

Both Abbey and Ryan turned to stare at Steve.

'Excuse me?' Ryan said. 'I practically had to blackmail you to get you here.'

Then it was Steve's turn to flush.

'Yeah, well, I'm enjoying myself,' he admitted sheepishly. 'Medicine's a bit dry when it's only books. I think I might be about to make another career change.'

'Well, how about a spot of nursing?' Eileen suggested. 'We're short a few, and doctors seem to be thick on the ground around here. Let's divvy up our patients, shall we? How will we work it? Draw straws?'

In the end they didn't need to. Abbey agreed she really only needed to visit Ian Miller and Janet to keep herself happy—then she'd go back to Jack and her cows. Ryan's father was due to be ambulanced back to Sapphire Cove within the next hour and Ryan wanted to be at the hospital when his father arrived. He volunteered for morning ward round. That left Steve free to read the morning newspapers and then take morning surgery.

Abbey went to see Janet, shaking her head in bewilderment. To have too many doctors...

Steve Pryor was thinking the same thing.

'You don't want to pay me off and have me leave, do you?' Steve asked Ryan as Abbey disappeared down the corridor. Steve's voice was a trifle anxious. 'I mean...you wanted me here for four weeks, right?'

'Yeah, well...' Ryan was watching Abbey walk away, and he hardly heard.

'Ryan, Abbey's coming back to work on Monday,' Steve went on slowly, following Ryan's gaze. 'I thought... Wasn't the idea that I'd help her out for a couple more weeks but we wouldn't see you here after Monday? You'll be off, getting married and looking after your dad.'

'That's right.' Ryan was still gazing at the now empty corridor.

Steve wasn't stupid. He was putting one and two together. Or one and one. And one and one makes two...

There was only one thing to do here. If you want to know something badly enough then ask. Steve squared his shoulders. And asked.

'Ryan, am I imagining things here, or do you fancy working with Abbey yourself?'

'What?' Ryan turned reluctantly to stare at Steve. 'No.'

'So...' Steve put his head on one side, considering. 'You just like the work—is that it?' The corners of his mouth twitched into a smile. 'Well, if that's the case, you won't mind if I ask Abbey out to dinner over the weekend.'

Ryan stared. 'You and Abbey...'

'Me and Abbey...'

'Hell!'

And then silence.

The corners of Steve's mouth curved all the way into laughter. He now knew all he needed to know.

'Gotcha,' he said lightly, and grinned. 'Don't worry, Ryan. In fact, there's a rather special nurse who works nights who's agreed to go out with me already. The date with Abbey line was a ruse. I just was getting vibes about you and Abbey, and thought I might put my vibes to the test.' His grin deepened to unholy enjoyment. 'And I was right.'

'Steve, there's nothing…' Ryan was fighting to gain control again. Steve Pryor was too intelligent for his own good. He saw too darned much. 'There's nothing between me and Abbey. Hell, Steve, I can't object to whoever you want to date. I'm engaged to Felicity. Remember?'

'Yeah, I remember,' Steve said dryly. 'If I were you I'd do something about that. It's likely to cause all manner of complications.'

Ian Miller looked grey.

Tucked into a side ward by himself, Ian had spent the night recovering from the effects of the gas. Ryan paused at the door and checked him over. It was no wonder he'd taken a chance and guessed AIDS. Ian might still be simply HIV positive and not have full-blown AIDS, but the man looked haggard.

Maybe he wasn't really ill, though, Ryan thought as he did a fast visual examination. Ian was thin but not to the point of emaciation. Underneath his fear there could well be a reasonably healthy male.

Ryan knocked lightly on the door and Ian hardly stirred. 'Hi, Ian. Finished breakfast?' Ryan checked Ian's barely touched tray and frowned. 'You want to talk?'

Ian looked up wearily from his pillows and shrugged.

'I'm here on ward round,' Ryan told him, hauling up a chair and lowering his long frame. 'As a good doctor, I should examine you—but I won't if you don't want. Any after-effects of the gas?'

'No.'

'Then just tell me where you're up to with your AIDS. I assume you have a definite diagnosis? We're not dealing with guesswork here? Full-blown AIDS or just HIV positive?'

'No guesswork.' Drearily Ian outlined his history. He'd heard a friend had died of AIDS so he'd had himself tested.

The HIV positive diagnosis had been confirmed a month ago.

'Just HIV? Not full-blown AIDS?'

'No.'

'Well, that's a bonus. Have you had any counselling?'

Ian shook his head. 'Hell, Ryan, I'm a lawyer,' he said bleakly. 'I don't need counselling. I've watched friends die in the past.'

'Hmm.' Ryan nodded. 'So...you tried suicide because you think you're going to die horribly and die soon.'

'Yeah, well, I would have died last night—'

'If we hadn't messed you around.' Ryan smiled as Abbey appeared at the door. 'Hey, Abbey, we're just being accused of interfering with this man's life. Or death. And he's a lawyer, for heaven's sake. Do you think he'll sue?'

'You'd better not,' Abbey said warmly. She crossed to Ian's bed, stooped and hugged Ian hard. 'If you do I'll tell your mother on you, Ian Miller, and she's a force to be reckoned with. Your mum's been worried sick, Ian. She guessed something was wrong way before this. I think you should have told her.'

'I can't.'

'Why not?'

Silence.

'Does your mother know you're gay?' Ryan asked, and Ian shook his head.

'No. That's why, well, I live in Sydney.'

'You don't think it might be kinder to tell her?'

'I don't want people here to know,' Ian said explosively. 'They're so damned judgemental.'

'They're not, you know,' Abbey said softly. 'I think you've forgotten all the good things about small towns, Ian

Miller. You and Ryan both. You left here when you were fifteen and seventeen respectively and you've hardly been back since. But Sapphire Cove... Well, one of the things it's really good at is protecting its own. You belong here, Ian. You won't be tarred or feathered by your family when they know.'

'How do you know?'

Abbey tilted her head. 'Well, for a start I'd imagine many of them have guessed you're gay already. Ryan had, and he's working on old memories. Maybe you're underestimating them. Tell them, and see if I'm not wrong.'

'But AIDS... Hell, Abbey, I'm not just confessing I'm gay. I have AIDS.'

'At the risk of repeating something that's been said time and time again, AIDS is a word. Not a sentence,' Abbey told him. 'You tell him about the current treatments, Ryan.'

'Ian, for a start you don't have AIDS,' Ryan said steadily, 'you're HIV positive. So just stop being so damned dramatic and negative and listen.'

Then Ryan outlined the treatments now favoured in the USA—and Abbey was stunned.

Ryan had certainly done his homework. This wasn't a brief description of AIDS treatments at the superficial level most doctors could give. Some time between the time Abbey had left Ryan last night and now, Ryan had read every piece of pertinent modern literature on the current treatments and prognoses for AIDS. Ian had a sharp lawyer's mind and he threw questions at Ryan almost faster than Abbey could think them up—and Ryan calmly answered every one.

'Look, mate, the information you're working on is years out of date,' he said firmly. 'The breakthrough in AIDS research has been monumental. You'll no longer be treated with just the one drug. There's a real mix. The side-effects of the combined therapies are minimal and life expectancy is increasing dramatically—to a stage now where the medical profession is refusing to make predictions on life expectancy at all.

'They're cautiously optimistic that in cases like yours, where you haven't converted to full-blown AIDS, then that conversion may never happen.'

'A couple of years ago we were saying life expectancy was up to five years,' he continued. 'Now…now we don't endline it at all. Every case is different. The life expectancy is stretching out and out and we're hopeful that many cases like yours will never develop at all into full-blown AIDS. There's millions being poured into AIDS funding and new breakthroughs are happening all the time.

'Maybe, well, just maybe, given the present rate of learning, you're more likely to get run over by a bus than to die in the next ten years from the disease you have.'

Ryan smiled.

'And that would have been a waste of a funeral if you'd happened to bump yourself off last night—now, wouldn't it?'

Ian stared at Ryan. His face was intent and fearful, as though he was afraid to let himself hope.

'You're kidding.'

'It's all here, mate.' Ryan produced page after page of copious notes. 'I thought you wouldn't believe me so I had a colleague fax through the literature.'

Ian stared up, unbelieving. He lifted the first sheet and read. Then the second. And then he lifted the whole pile. Some of the greyness eased from his face, and all of a sudden he looked lighter and younger. A life sentence had just been lifted—and he might just choose to live.

His face clouded again.

'My job, though,' he said fretfully. 'I'm a corporate lawyer for an international company. We're required to have a full medical every year as part of our superannuation scheme. When they know, there's no way they'll keep me on.'

'Then quit,' Ryan said promptly—so promptly that Abbey blinked.

'Yeah? And do what?'

'Do an Abbey.' Ryan looked across to Abbey and his

smile gentled. 'Hell, Ian, while you and I have been out in the big wide world, making our millions, Abbey's been here holding Sapphire Cove together with a piece of string. And the locals love her for it. I've been asking around this morning about lawyers in Sapphire Cove. There's one. He's about eighty and is capable of signing affidavits if someone holds his wrist and the magnifying glass—and that's the extent of it.

'If you were to come back... Well, like Abbey, the locals would fall on your neck and ask questions later. Maybe it'd work long term and maybe it wouldn't, but in the short term I think Sapphire Cove might be just what you need.'

'Come back...'

'I don't see why you shouldn't—at least for a while,' Ryan said. 'You're emotionally and physically exhausted. It doesn't take Abbey's or my medical qualifications to tell us that. You've been living a nightmare, and a stressful corporate job with an axe hanging over your head isn't what you need. So why not come home for a while and see if Sapphire Cove can't work its magic on you?' He smiled. 'Ian, Abbey and I saw a turtle laying her eggs last night. Why don't you stick around and see those eggs hatch?'

'A turtle?' Ian pushed himself up on his pillows. Like Ryan and Abbey and most kids around Sapphire Cove, Ian had done his own turtle-hunting. His eyes lit up like magic. 'Where?'

'A mile south of where we found you, filling yourself with exhaust fumes. If you like, I'll run you out later and show you.'

Ian stared, and then let the doubt creep back. 'You don't have to do that. Hell, Ryan, I don't need patronising.'

'And I don't need humouring,' Ryan said mildly. 'If you don't want to come then say so. I'm going out to check anyway. I'll stick my head in here when I leave and see if you're up to a drive.' His smile faded and he fixed Ian with a challenging look. 'Now, Abbey and I have work to do and you need to think. Any questions?'

'Maybe in a while,' Ian told him slowly. He stared down at the sheaf of papers on his bed. 'When I've read this.'

'We'll leave you to it, then,' Ryan told him. 'Take it that we'll discharge you when you've summarised the lot!'

'For heaven's sake, Ryan, you sounded almost home-sick,' Abbey told him as they left the room together. 'Talking Ian into coming back here to work…'

'If he agrees it'd be the best thing for him.'

'But he's a corporate lawyer. His mum says he spends half his life overseas on one international deal after another. How could someone like that be happy in Sapphire Cove?'

Abbey glanced uncertainly at Ryan. She'd once known this man so well, and now she knew him hardly at all. He'd sounded convincing in there, talking Ian into a life in Sapphire Cove. Yet… Yet Ryan had left it without a backward glance.

'Ian's like you,' she said softly. 'He's left here, Ryan, and I don't think you can come back again. To be content with Sapphire Cove after you've seen the big wide world…' She shrugged. 'Well, you'd know how hard that could be.'

Silence.

Ryan didn't answer. For the life of him, he couldn't think of a single thing to say.

Abbey looked at him for a long moment—and then turned away from his side to go and visit Janet.

Sam Henry arrived back at Sapphire Cove an hour later, and within two minutes of arriving he demanded to see Janet.

'You don't think we should get you settled into a ward and give you a rest first?' Ryan asked doubtfully. Sam had come though the operation with flying colours. Now ten days post-op, he was looking good but it was a long ambulance drive from Cairns.

'Nope.' Sam reached out and gripped Ryan's arm. The ambulance officers were standing at each end of his trolley, waiting for directions, and Sam knew exactly where he wanted to go. 'But it's good to see you still here, Ryan. You're not married yet, I hope?'

'I told you we'd wait for you to get back before we tied the knot.'

'Good. The wedding's not this afternoon?'

'No. I'll bring Felicity in to see you this afternoon and we'll talk about setting a time.'

'Good.' Sam smiled in satisfaction. 'It's not organised yet, then. I'm not up to a wedding for a few days at least. But Janet…' The hand gripping Ryan's tightened in anxiety. 'I need to see her. You said she was fine?'

'She's fine. She's only three days post-op, though, Dad, and she's pretty sore.'

'Not up to receiving visitors?' There was apprehension in Sam's voice and Ryan frowned down at him.

'She can have visitors, I guess. If it's important we'll take you there now.'

'That's what I want.' Sam fell back on his pillows, folded his arms across his chest and prepared to be wheeled on. 'Take me away, boys. I've got a mended heart here, and I'm raring to go.'

'Why do you suppose my father wants to see your mother-in-law so badly?' Ryan demanded. He'd tracked Abbey down in Sister's station and found her writing medico-legal letters. 'And just what do you think you're doing?'

'Catching up on some paperwork,' Abbey said mildly. 'Marcia told me she'd look after Jack until lunchtime and it seemed too good an opportunity to miss.' She hesitated. 'I guess as soon as you and Steve leave I'll go back to chasing my tail again. I don't want to start from behind.'

'No.'

There was silence while Ryan thought about Abbey chasing her tail with overwork again.

And thought about leaving her for good.

'Sam's back, then?' Abbey asked lightly, searching Ryan's face. It seemed set and forbidding.

'He arrived ten minutes ago. And the first thing he demanded was to see Janet.' Ryan's frown deepened. 'Abbey, am I imagining things here? Do you think there's anything between the pair of them?'

'They've always been good friends,' Abbey told him. She hesitated. 'Like you and me,' she added, her voice slightly hesitant. 'They were kids together. That sort of thing.'

'So there couldn't be any sort of romantic attachment?'

'I told you,' Abbey said heavily. 'It's like you and me. Friends. That's all.' She searched for some way to change the subject, and her eyes rested on her pile of patient notes. Leith Kinley…as good a topic as any.

'I saw Leith's dad this morning,' she told Ryan, her words sounding stiff and forced. 'He stopped me outside the hospital as I arrived. He just wanted to tell me how well Leith was going with her swimming. I didn't know you'd been taking her for more swimming lessons.'

'Yeah, well…' Ryan shrugged. 'She's a good kid. I'm enjoying teaching her.'

'I would have thought…' Abbey bit her lip but the words came out anyway. 'Ryan, are you spending any time at all with Felicity? She must be bored stupid—with all the help you've been giving me, the time you spend with your dad and now Leith…'

'Felicity's not bored,' Ryan said coldly.

'Well, if it was my honeymoon you'd hijacked I'd be really cross,' Abbey said frankly. 'And if she knew you'd been kissing me last night…' She swallowed and stopped in mid-sentence, the thought of kissing Ryan last night flooding back with dizzying intensity.

But what she had to say must be said. Ryan had been so generous to her. He'd given her his honeymoon, but that honeymoon also belonged to Felicity.

'Ryan, if you're not careful you'll mess up your marriage because of me,' she said softly. 'And I don't think you want to do that.'

'Abbey…'

'I need to work now, Ryan,' Abbey said dully.

'Please…leave me alone to do that. I think you should go back to Felicity.'

After that, Ryan finished doing his ward round, which had been interrupted by Sam's arrival, and tried to get his thoughts in order.

Abbey was right. He wasn't being fair to Felicity.

Hell, he'd thought Felicity would have been bored stupid by now. He'd thought Felicity wouldn't have stayed.

But Felicity seemed to have an endless supply of work at the end of her modem and was perfectly happy to base herself at Sam's house while he helped Abbey.

While he helped Abbey…

There was no longer any need for him to help Abbey, he conceded as he changed the dressing on little Peter Harknet's burned foot. The local farmers were still milking Abbey's cows, despite her protestations, and they would until Janet was up and around again. Abbey had herself a decent babysitter. Her knee was almost back to normal and for the next two weeks Steve was here to make her work-load reasonable.

So…

So Ryan should just slope on back to Felicity.

He was like Steve. He didn't want to.

'How come you're not talking?' Pete demanded as Ryan cleaned down the burned area of his foot and applied cream. Five-year-old Pete had burned himself by sticking his toes into a box of dry ice which had been keeping his birthday ice-cream cake cold. He'd been in Children's ward for three days. Normally he chattered like a butcher's magpie, and Ryan's silence wasn't to his taste. 'Cat got your tongue?' he demanded.

'No.' Ryan managed a smile. 'Sorry, mate. I'm just thinking. I'm just thinking what a really dumb thing it is to stick your toes in places to see what it feels like.'

'I was going to taste some,' Pete informed him. 'Just lucky I didn't do that, eh? Mum says I would have burned the tongue right out of my head!'

'Very lucky,' Ryan agreed. 'Pete, if you live till you're ten it'll be a miracle.'

'My mum says you're getting married real soon,' Pete went on, unperturbed. Then he winced. 'Yike. That hurt.'

Ryan winced too. The dead skin was coming away as he gently cleaned it. The procedure was impossible to do without hurting at all. Pete was a really brave little patient.

He deserved to have all his attention.

'That's right.'

'You're marrying a lady from America?'

'Yep.'

Pete screwed up his nose. 'You sound a bit American but you're really from Sapphire Cove—right?'

'Well, yes. But that was a long time ago.'

'Then why don't you marry someone from here and live here again like we do,' Pete announced. 'Why d'ya want to go away for?'

Why, indeed.

Silence.

'Cat got your tongue?' Pet demanded, and Ryan could only nod agreement.

Ian Miller didn't have time to go with him to see where the turtle had laid her eggs. Ryan went back to Ian's ward when he'd finished his rounds and found him surrounded by family.

Masses of family. Mother, brothers, sisters, nieces, nephews, brothers-in-law…the whole box and dice. And somewhere in the midst of them was Ian, being absorbed again into the clan.

Ian looked through the crowd and met Ryan's eyes—and grinned. The greyness in his face was receding by the minute.

'Out, you lot,' he ordered his family. 'Here's my doctor and I want to ask him if you guys can take me home.'

When the family had receded just outside the door Ian hopped out of bed and closed it firmly against them. And grinned again.

'You'd think they owned me.'

Ryan smiled back. 'You've told them?'

'Yep.'

'And you haven't been cast out of the family?'

'No.' Ian's smile faded. He sank onto the bed again. The toll of the last few weeks' emotional turmoil and his brush with death the night before had left him weak, but there was a determination in his eyes which was growing by the minute. 'Abbey...Dr Wittner was right,' he said. 'The family already knew I was gay. They hadn't talked about it because they'd decided it was my business and I'd talk about it if I wanted it talked about. Typical, really. My family...'

'They want to help?'

'They sure do.' Ian shook his head, his voice laced with wonder. 'I told them I was HIV positive and my sisters started berating me for not laying it on them and for not trusting them. My mother burst into tears and fell on my neck.

'And my brothers-in-law told me I was a cloth-head and that your idea of me practising law here was the best one they'd heard for a long time. The general consensus was that I'd be a darn sight more use practising law in Sapphire Cove than pushing up daisies. Which I'm starting to think—'

'Might be true,' Ryan finished for him. 'Hell, mate, you can only give it a go. Get yourself on a firm footing again, get your medical regime established and then see if you want to face the world outside Sapphire Cove again.'

Ryan looked out the window across the headland. The sea was a wide band of sparkling sapphire against the horizon. 'Sapphire Cove really is the loveliest place in the world to live,' he said, and his voice was tinged with regret.

'How come you don't live here any more, then?' Ian asked, and Ryan shrugged.

'I'm still on a career path,' he said with some reluctance. 'I have commitments in the States that it'd take more than AIDS to shift, and I have a fiancée who couldn't live here

in a fit. No. I wish you all the best here, mate, but I'm
afraid I have to go.'

The turtle eggs were safe.

Ryan should have been back at home with Felicity.
Instead, he spent the next two hours sitting on the beach,
watching the barren sweep of sand where last night the
turtle had laid her eggs. The tide had done its job well.
There was now almost no sign that underneath the sand
there were scores of tiny turtles growing towards life.

How long did they take to hatch?

Heaven knew. Ryan didn't. And he didn't want to know.
He didn't want to be back in the States, look down at his
calendar and say, 'Today's the day half Sapphire Cove will
be out, escorting baby turtles to the water.'

He had to go back.

There was nothing for him here, he told himself.
Nothing. Sure, Sapphire Cove was a beautiful place, but he
hadn't fought his way up the career ladder to abandon it
now—abandon it on a whim.

Abandon it because he wanted to please Abbey?

The thought of Abbey was overpowering. He couldn't
get her out of his thoughts. The feel of her last night...her
soft curves yielding to his touch...the scent of her...her
lovely dusky curls against his face...

Abbey...

Dear God, he wanted her. Ryan shifted uneasily on the
sand and finally rose. He walked down to the water's edge
and stood, looking out to sea, as if the answers could somehow be found out there.

They couldn't. Of course they couldn't.

He had to go home. To the States. He had to marry
Felicity.

No.

He couldn't marry Felicity. He couldn't.

Last night Felicity had kissed him goodnight deeply—
passionately. If the phone hadn't demanded her attention
she would have wanted to make love.

And Ryan hadn't wanted to make love one bit. Not with Felicity. Back in the States he had thought of Felicity as one of the most beautiful women he knew. Powerful. Ambitious. Wonderful.

All the adjectives he'd used were still true, except the 'wonderful'. He no longer wanted to marry someone who spent her life attached to a mobile phone and a computer.

He wanted to marry Abbey.

The thought settled into his mind like a flaming arrow and it buried itself into his heart and burned.

Marry Abbey.

If he married Abbey then he'd already have a son. He and Felicity had talked of children and had decided against them. It wasn't that either of them disliked them. It was just that they hardly felt they had time for them.

But Jack...

Ryan thought back to the flaming-haired toddler, demanding more egg to be aeroplaned into his mouth. Wobbling on his sturdy little legs. His head upended in a pudding bowl. And Ryan's mouth curved into a smile. It'd be no problem at all to have Jack. Maybe adopt him, if Abbey didn't object.

And Abbey... Well, she could be a full-time mum. She'd like that. Give her a chance to be looked after for a change.

How would she like New York?

A flash of doubt swept through his mind at the thought of Abbey in New York, but he suppressed it fast. The thought of Abbey as his wife was so, well, so tantalising...

It had to be possible.

Convincing Abbey would be the easy part.

What came before was the hard part.

Telling Felicity he'd made an awful mistake.

CHAPTER TEN

'You have to be kidding!'

As a reaction to a marriage proposal, Abbey's first words left a bit to be desired, Ryan thought. Still, maybe it was no more than he deserved.

He'd asked Abbey to marry him in her dairy.

Ryan had come to Abbey's that evening, expecting to find her resting and with Jack in bed. Instead, he'd discovered she'd told the local farmers who'd been milking her cows that she was fine by herself. Jack had been given his dinner and his mother had discussed bedtime with him but Jack had had a long afternoon nap and had been in no mood for sleep. He'd been making mud pies in a play-pen in a corner of the dairy and Abbey had been milking her thirteenth cow.

'What do you want?' she'd demanded when Ryan had come through the dairy gate and had startled Abbey's cows in the process. The herd had then twitched and become nervous and had made Abbey's job hard.

Ryan had been thrown so far off balance that he'd told Abbey what he'd wanted, straight out.

'I'm not marrying Felicity any more,' he'd said flatly. 'I want you.'

As a proposal it had lacked a little finesse, he told himself later. Abbey's reaction had confirmed it.

'You have to be kidding.'

She reached up and patted her cow's rump, settled herself again and kept right on milking.

'No, Ryan, stay over there,' she ordered, as he took a couple of steps nearer. 'My girls don't like strangers. I know you milked them once but they don't remember you. Or maybe they do and it's that that's making them nervous.' She frowned, and he couldn't see by her face what

145

she was thinking. 'So tell me. What have you done with your Felicity?'

'I haven't done anything with Felicity,' Ryan said, exasperated. 'But she's no longer *my* Felicity. She's gone home. Abbey, can you leave your damned cows for a minute?'

'Not while Jack's being so good.' Abbey smiled sweetly and only she knew the effort her nonchalance cost her. 'I'm on my thirteenth cow. Why don't you go in and make us a cup of tea while you wait for me?'

Ryan almost ground his teeth. 'Abbey, I want to speak to you. Damn it, Abbey, I want to marry you.'

Abbey looked over to Ryan for a long, long moment. Then she sighed, her nonchalance slipping. 'You know, Ryan, I'm almost sure you don't.' She rose, tipped her bucket of milk into the waiting vat and went to bring in another cow.

Ryan waited.

Silence.

Abbey roped her next cow into the bail and sighed.

'Ryan, this is crazy,' she told him. 'Go inside and put the kettle on and I'll be with you in fifteen minutes.'

And she turned her back on him and started milking her fourteenth cow.

Abbey had full need of those fifteen minutes. Her head was spinning.

She'd managed to keep her voice calm, she told herself proudly, but it had taken a Herculean effort. To keep calm when Ryan had asked a question like that...

'I want you,' he'd said.

Well, that much she'd known already. Last night Ryan had wanted Abbey and Abbey had wanted him. Their reaction to each other on the beach had been pure animal longing.

That's what it was. Lust. Nothing more, she told herself flatly. Nothing.

But Ryan must have thought it more than that. Today he'd sent Felicity away.

Poor Felicity.

Abbey looked over to where Jack was squeezing mud through his fingers. He was totally engrossed in the rich black mire, sliming through onto his bare knees. Abbey had provided him with a whole bucket of mud and it promised to keep him good for another hour or more. He was dressed only in a nappy and he was filthy.

One of the cows who'd already been milked had doubled back to watch the little boy. The cow hung over Jack's play-pen, her kindly bovine face watching Jack with interest.

Jack reached up and put one grimy finger on her nose—and shouted with laughter at the black splodge on her brown velvety face.

This place—this lifestyle—was about as far from New York as life could possibly get.

But Ryan had just asked her to marry him.

Good grief! Abbey's overwhelming sensation was shock. Sure, Ryan had kissed her last night. Sure, she was head over heels in love with the man. But…marriage?

Marriage to Ryan was so far out of the realm of possibility that Abbey had never dreamed of it. Or maybe she had dreamed, but in the way someone in New York would fantasise about life in a tropical paradise. A dream. Nothing more.

Marriage to Ryan meant life as a New York consultant's wife. Life away from here.

No and no and no.

But…marriage to Ryan…

To be with Ryan was all she wanted, Abbey told herself bleakly. Marriage to Ryan was the fitting together of two halves of a whole. But…

No way! There was no way in the wide world she could marry Ryan. She wasn't just Abbey Wittner any longer. She was Janet's daughter-in-law and Jack's mother, and also Sapphire Cove's doctor. A lone and independent Abbey might marry Ryan and adjust to life at his side on the other side of the world. But Jack's mum couldn't.

Janet's daughter-in-law couldn't. John's widow, who still had debts to pay, couldn't.

Sapphire Cove's only doctor couldn't.

So Abbey blinked back tears of depression—and kept right on milking. Damn Ryan Henry. Why did he have to come back here in the first place?

'Abbey, you must marry me.'

Abbey was hardly through the kitchen door before Ryan threw his line at her.

Abbey blanched.

Damn. Ryan bit his tongue in disgust as he saw her recoil. This wasn't Ryan at his persuasive best. He was way out of line here—thrown right off balance. It seemed there was only one thought in his head.

Marriage to Abbey…

After his visit to the turtle eggs he'd gone back to Felicity, to find her pacing his father's farmhouse.

'Where the hell have you been?'

When he hadn't answered she'd supplied the answer for him.

'You've been with that girl, haven't you?'

'No, I—'

He'd got no further. Felicity had picked up his lap-top computer—*his*, mind, not her precious machine—and had hurled it straight at him. It had missed and slammed into the wall.

And had smashed.

'You've wasted my time, Ryan Henry,' she snarled. 'I ought to sue you. Two damned weeks I've spent kicking my heels…'

'Hey, half that time was spent in Hawaii.'

'I could have stayed in Hawaii. Do you know how many meetings I've missed? All because of you.'

'Felicity…'

'Even if you weren't with that girl, I'm still sick of it,' she snapped. 'I've been so patient I can't believe it. I've sat here and waited while you ran round after your goddammed father and I haven't said a word while you operated in this God-forsaken hospital and worried about that girl's damned cows...

'And then I rang the hospital, looking for you, and got someone called Ted who sounds like a morgue attendant and he said maybe you'd gone out and killed yourself on the road because it seemed to be in fashion to knock yourself off. And then he changed his mind and said it was more likely you were out making love to Abbey Wittner. And he even said that it was a shame if you weren't feeling suicidal because he needs a good death to keep up the occupancy rate of his damned morgue...'

She stopped, exasperated, as Ryan's mouth twitched into a smile. 'No. Don't you dare laugh, Ryan. I've had enough. Whether you were with her or not, I don't care. I'm not staying. This whole place is crazy and if I stay one minute longer it'll infect me.' She paused for breath.

'Ryan, there's an urgent meeting tomorrow afternoon in New York. They've just e-mailed me and I must be there.' She hesitated for a whole ten seconds—and then hauled the diamond from her left hand. 'I'm going, but I don't think you want me to take this with me—do you Ryan?'

'Felicity...'

'I don't want to take it,' she confided, softening a little and pressing it into his hand. 'Ryan, I decided to marry you because you knew where you were going in life. Now...well, you're vacillating, and I can't stand it.' She reached out and kissed his forehead. 'Goodbye, Ryan.' Then she stared down at his smashed computer and it was her turn to smile. 'And I hope I crashed your hard disk.'

That was the end of Felicity.

And all Ryan could think of as he watched her pack and leave was that now he was free to talk to Abbey.

And now, here was Abbey, standing at the kitchen door in filthy overalls and gum boots and her toddler in her arms dripping mud.

His one thought kept echoing. 'Abbey, you must marry me.'

Abbey didn't answer. She simply held Jack out to him, and before he knew it Ryan had a splodge of muddy baby in his arms.

'You bath him while I take a shower and then I'll make us both an omelette,' she said.

'Abbey…'

'I refuse to cope with perfectly ridiculous requests on an empty stomach.'

'It's not a perfectly ridiculous request.'

'Wash my son and then we'll talk about it.'

Washing Jack was not as easy as it looked. In fact, it took three rinses before the water ran clean. Jack thoroughly enjoyed the whole experience. The only part he didn't enjoy was getting dressed again. Ryan finally gave up and came out into the kitchen, carrying a naked toddler in one arm and a nappy in the other.

'OK. You win. I need a mother here.'

Abbey was clean herself. There was a cold shower on the back verandah. She'd thrown herself under it in the hope it might shake some sense into her head, and then hauled on jeans and a T-shirt.

She should be cool. Instead, she was as hot and flustered as she'd ever been in her life.

Keep it light, Abbey told herself. Keep it…keep it away from heartbreak.

'You mean you can cope with the intricacies of microsurgery but not a piece of flannel?'

'That's right.'

'Wuss!'

It was *so* hard to keep her voice light.

She had the makings of omelette on the table. Now she took her naked son from Ryan, and pointed to the eggs.

'OK, if you can't do nappies you're on omelette duty.'

Ryan blinked.

'Hell, Abbey, I can't cook.'

'Why not?'

'I've never learned. I have a housekeeper.'

'A housekeeper? Back in New York?'

'Well, yes…'

'And if I married you would I have a housekeeper?' Abbey asked carefully.

'I guess… Yeah, of course you would. Mrs O'Hara could look after Jack…'

'While I went out to work?'

'Abbey, I don't know about registration in the States,' Ryan admitted. 'It's been easier for me here because I have Australian citizenship. I'll have to look into whether you need to retrain or not. Registration could take some time.' He spread his hands. 'But, hell, Abbey, you've worked so hard all your life… Why don't you marry me and let me take care of you for a while?'

'I wouldn't know how to,' Abbey confessed. 'Ryan, just hold on here.' She hugged her small naked son against her, as if he gave her strength. 'This morning you were engaged to Felicity. Right?'

'Right, but—'

'But you're not engaged to her now?'

'No.'

'Why not?'

'Because we don't love one another.' Ryan wanted to lunge over and take Abbey in his arms. Make her feel like he was feeling. Desperate to have her close. But it was a bit hard to lunge at a woman with a naked baby hugged to her breast.

Abbey closed her eyes. 'You decided that today, then? That you don't love Felicity? Just like that?'

'Abbey, Felicity and I have never loved each other,' Ryan said slowly, pushing back the urge to lunge. 'Admired and respected each other—yes. Thought we were compatible—yes. I thought I'd be proud to call Felicity my wife and she felt the same about me. But marriage to each other was something that suited us. It would have made no demands on our lifestyles. It would have fitted in.'

'And now…'

'I've discovered that it's not enough,' Ryan said simply. 'I want you.'

'I see.'

Silence.

Abbey turned away to a couch by the stove, bent over and started putting a nappy on her son. Ryan watched in silence as Jack submitted to his nappy with no trouble at all.

Finally respectable, Jack was set on his feet to toddle out to the verandah. The sun was setting in the west over the mountains. The hens were starting to roost and Jack headed off toward the henhouses to watch his friends put themselves to bed.

As if Ryan wasn't there, Abbey wandered out to watch, her idea of cooking omelettes forgotten. Ryan followed.

'Marriage…' Abbey whispered. She put her hands on the weathered verandah rail and looked out over her run-down farm. 'You really want to marry me?'

'I do.' Ryan came up behind her and put his hands on her shoulders. Touching her felt so good. So right. He wanted to swing her around and pull her into his arms but he knew instinctively that she would resist. She wasn't ready.

Her body was tense beneath his hands.

'Ryan, you don't want to stay here,' she whispered.

'No. Of course not.' Ryan's grip tightened. 'My work's important. Hell, Abbey, I make more in a week in New York than I think you make in a year. We can both be comfortable on my income. Jack can go to any school he wants. He can have everything. We can have more children…' He did turn her then so she was facing him against the setting sun.

'Abbey, I love you,' he said softly, and he tilted her chin so she was forced to look up at him. 'I think I always have. I didn't want to leave when I was fifteen, and I should have come back before this. I never realised I'd left something so precious behind.'

'And now you've realised you'll pick it up and take it away…take me back to New York?'

'If you'll come.' He stooped to kiss her but Abbey pulled back, her eyes searching his in the soft twilight.

'Ryan, no…' She fended him off, pushing him away with her hands, and the feel of his heartbeat under her palms made her want to cry. What she had to say was so hard.

That she wasn't just Abbey. She was Jack's mum. Janet's daughter-in-law. Sapphire Cove's doctor.

'Ryan, what you said about you and Felicity, fitting into each other's lifestyles—it may not be the most important thing about a marriage but it's important, all the same.'

'You'd fit.' He took her waist and pulled her into his arms but she still resisted. 'Believe me, Abbey, you'd fit.'

'Maybe,' she whispered. 'Maybe I'd fit into your lifestyle. But maybe I wouldn't be happy, fitting into your lifestyle. And I can't see you fitting into mine.'

'Abbey…' Ryan looked down into her troubled eyes. 'Hell, sweetheart…' He lifted a hand from her waist and gestured around him. 'You can't live like this for the rest of your life. In debt, and up to your ears in work.'

'No. But I can't live like you want me to either,' she said sadly. 'In wealth and up to my ears in idleness.'

'Abbey, I want to look after you.'

'Yeah, well, I'm not ten years old now, Ryan Henry,' she snapped, and suddenly hauled herself back from him. He was being obtuse here. Thick! 'I'm twenty-eight years old and I'm a doctor and… I know it sounds pious, Ryan, but here people need me. Jack needs me. Janet and Sam need me. Sapphire Cove needs me. I'm not going to walk away. And I think…'

She took a deep breath and desolation welled up all around her. 'I think Jack needs to grow up here. His grandma's here. There are people here who loved his daddy. If I took him away it'd be like cutting him off from his father's memory for ever. And I can't do that.'

'Abbey…'

'Please, Ryan…' Her voice was desolate. 'Don't. All I want to do is come with you.' She looked up at him, her eyes bright with tears. 'I love you, Ryan Henry,' she admitted. 'I want you more than anything in the world. But…but, Ryan, I've only just found my turtle. I have to stay.'

He did lunge then. The sight of her…small and defenceless and desolate, standing there in her bare feet on floorboards that threatened to rot away underneath her. To leave her…

Before she could protest he gathered her into his arms and he held her close, moulding her body to his. He kissed the top of her head and she buried her face in his chest to stop him kissing her anywhere else.

'Ryan, don't… Please…'

'Abbey, I must. This is nonsense. We can take Janet with us. You'll have Janet and Jack. And we'll come back. I promise. We'll return for a month every year so Jack can learn to love this place and I can spend time with my father.'

Ryan's hands caressed the small of her back and he pressed her to him with such tenderness that Abbey almost said yes.

It would be so easy. All her problems solved by uttering one word.

She couldn't say it.

She stood with her face pressed against the soft fabric of Ryan's shirt and she felt his heart beating against hers. This was her home. This was right.

But nothing else was.

New York. Housekeepers. Luxury.

The little hospital here would close without a permanent doctor. Sam would break his heart. Janet would refuse to come and would be alone.

And Jack would have to wear shoes and not play in mud, and when he grew up a little he wouldn't be able to search for turtles.

Turtles.

In a little while the turtles, buried safe under the sand, would hatch and make their way down to the sea. Abbey knew that the whole town would turn out to watch. She'd take Jack to see and then, maybe then, the hard work and the poverty would be paid for.

Ryan said he earned more in a week than she did in a year. Maybe. But her payment was something you couldn't measure in dollars.

Living in Sapphire Cove was a heritage for her son. Living here was companionship for Sam's and Janet's old age.

And it was turtles.

'I can't marry you, Ryan Henry,' Abbey said sadly, and her voice was so muffled against his chest that he had to bend his head to hear. 'I can't marry you because you don't have turtles in New York.'

And it was a measure of Ryan's love for her that he knew exactly what she meant.

And he knew he couldn't make her change her mind.

CHAPTER ELEVEN

'You love him.'

Janet was standing beside her bed, leaning heavily on her walking-frame. A week post-op, she was recovering brilliantly. Janet thought rehabilitation hospitals were for wimps—definitely not for the likes of Janet Wittner—so rehabilitation had to come to her. Ryan had organised a walking race—two waist-high bars about five yards long and a couple of feet apart—to be installed in the hospital corridor for her to practise her walking.

Abbey intended to supervise her practice. Now Janet took three halting steps towards her race, supported with her walking frame, and then she paused and turned back to where Abbey was standing by her bed.

Janet's eyes were troubled.

'Don't think I can't see what's eating you, girl,' she said gently. 'Every day you've been coming here the shadows under your eyes have been growing. With that nice Dr Pryor helping out at the hospital and Ryan Henry putting his oar in as well, you're more rested than you've been for years. But still the shadows...'

'I've been worried about you,' Abbey told her, a touch of defiance in her voice, and Janet snorted.

'Pull the other leg, Abbey. The new hip your Ryan's given me is working almost as well as the old one already. In a couple of weeks I'll be as good as new. Better.' And then Janet frowned. 'You're not worried about me in other ways, I hope? You're not worried about me being on my own if you marry your Ryan?'

Abbey winced. 'Janet, that's crazy. He's not...he's not my Ryan.'

'No? That fiancée of his has left him to go back to America. He doesn't seem to be pining one bit, and the way he looks at you... Abbey, has he asked you to marry him?'

And, at the look on Abbey's face, Janet's frown deepened.

'He has,' she announced softly in a voice of discovery. 'And you've told him no. I can see it in your face. Abbey, for heaven's sake, why did you say no? It's almost two years since John died. If I, as John's mother, think it's time you got a new life for yourself then surely you should too.' Her eyes perused Abbey's face with care. 'Abbey, you love Ryan Henry,' she said slowly. 'You love him. So why refuse to marry him?'

Abbey shook her head, but Janet's eyes didn't leave her face. She stood, waiting for an answer, and Abbey had to find one.

'Janet, I must refuse him,' Abbey said at last. 'What choice do I have?' She dug her hands deep into the pockets of her white coat, as though her doctor's uniform were some sort of security. 'Janet, Ryan wants me to be a New York consultant's wife. How on earth can I be that?' She bit her lip. 'I'm a doctor in my own right. I fought hard to be what I am.'

'You'll be what you are if you're here or if you're on the other side of the world,' Janet said brusquely. 'You'll be just the same Abbey. Only you'll be with Ryan.'

'No.' Abbey shook her head. 'I won't be. Janet, Ryan doesn't even know whether I can get registration. He doesn't know if I can work. And he doesn't see...he doesn't see that it's important.'

'Is it important?'

'You know it is.' Abbey crossed to the window and stared out over the headland to the sea beyond. 'Janet, this hospital...I fought so hard for it. We need it. Sapphire Cove needs it. I can't just walk away.'

'Not even with Ryan?'

Abbey shook her head.

'I love Ryan, but that's not all there is in the world,' she said. 'Just like my medicine's important but it's not everything. Jack... My little Jack would have to wear shoes. He'd lose his people.' She flung herself around so she was facing Janet again. 'Ryan says you could come with us. Would you want to come?'

'What—me in New York?' Janet's face sagged in astonishment. 'You have to be joking. I was born in Sapphire Cove and I'll die in Sapphire Cove, thank you very much. The thought of big cities fills me with the heebie-jeebies.'

'Same here,' Abbey told her, and tried to smile. 'So, you see? It's impossible. Crazy.'

'And yet you're breaking your heart to go with him.'

'It broke my heart when John died,' Abbey said bleakly. 'And yet here I am two years later, discussing marrying someone else. Life goes on. I'll live.' She stirred herself and crossed to hold the door open for Janet. 'Enough talk. Let's get you out to the race and get you walking. When all else fails, Janet Wittner, there's always work.'

There was more than that, Abbey thought as she and Eileen took Janet carefully through her exercises. More than just work in her life. There was this place, a wonderful nursing staff, her little son, Janet...

So why did life still seem so bleak?

'You're in love with Abbey Wittner!'

Sam Henry had one sock on and one sock off. Now he paused in his attempts to dress himself and fixed his son with a glare.

'I'm right, aren't I, boy? You're in love with our Abbey.'

'Dad, if you want me to take you out to see where these turtle eggs are incubating then let's keep the talk impersonal. Otherwise I might cut and run.'

'Like you and your mother did twenty years ago?'

'Dad...'

'Your mother didn't like getting involved,' Sam said darkly. 'That's why she hated it here. Hated Sapphire Cove. She should never have agreed to marry me in the first place.' Sam hauled his shoes on and gave his hand to his son to help him up. Although Sam was recovering well, he was still weak at the knees and breathless. In a few days he'd go home, but this was a first. An outing with Ryan, and then back to hospital at the end of it.

'You thinking of marrying her?' he demanded bluntly.

'Dad...'

'There's no use telling me to mind my own business,' Sam told him. 'You're my son—remember? So tell me. Your fiancée's sloped off back to New York and you're carrying a ring around with no one to give it to—right? So you're thinking of marrying our Abbey.' He steadied on his feet but he didn't relinquish his grip on his son. 'You could do worse, Ryan. Abbey's a damned fine girl.'

'I know she is,' Ryan said heavily. And then he shrugged. Talking to his father about his personal life was new to him, but he liked the sensation. It was just, well, hard to get used to.

And it was uncomfortable, talking about Abbey.

'Dad, I have asked her to marry me,' he confessed.

Sam stared. 'Yeah?' His whole face lightened. 'You and Abbey... Well, well.'

'She's refused.'

Sam frowned.

'Why on earth? Ryan, Janet tells me she's nuts about you.'

'Janet says... Dad, have you and Janet been talking about us?'

'You have to do something in this dratted hospital if you're not to go stir-crazy,' Sam retorted. 'Between bed-pans and library trolleys and people making you do a damned stupid set of exercises, talking to Janet's been a lifeline. And she's worried about that girl of hers. Says she's breaking her heart over you.'

'Not so you'd notice,' Ryan said morosely. 'She won't marry me.'

'Hell, why not?' Sam's face was still eager. 'Maybe it's just she needs time to get used to the idea. Ryan, it'd be great.' He took a deep breath. 'Tell you what. If it'll help, I'll buy a little place down closer to the beach and let you kids have the homestead. It's too big for me and it'd be a great place to bring up kids. That is...' he was watching Ryan's bleak face '...if you want more kids.'

But Ryan shook his head. 'Dad, that's more than generous, but you must see... Even if Abbey marries me we couldn't live here.'

Silence.

'Why not?' Sam asked at last, but the light had faded from his face as if it had never been.

'Because my life is in New York,' Ryan said explosively. 'Hell, Dad, I have a career.'

'And Abbey doesn't?'

'Well, yes, but what sort of career? It pays peanuts and you know it.'

'Maybe Abbey's content with peanuts,' Sam said sadly.

'How can she be?' Ryan demanded, and it was as if he was talking to himself. 'She works herself into the ground for nothing. But the lifestyle I'm offering her... I could look after her. Take her away from all this.'

'But Abbey loves "all this".' Sam's face softened. 'And, Ryan, so should you. You were born here. This is your heritage too.'

Ryan stared at him in astonishment. 'Dad, are you seriously suggesting that I should stay here?'

'If you want Abbey.'

'If Abbey loves me then she'll come with me.'

'No.' Sam shook his head. 'Abbey's not that selfish.'

'Selfish?'

'Abbey could go with you tomorrow—Janet tells me that—and be content. Heck, Ryan, Abbey's been your other half since she was knee-high to a grasshopper. The two of you are meant for each other. But she won't abandon her responsibilities, and you can't ask her to.'

'It's not like Sapphire Cove owns her.'

'No,' Sam said sadly. 'It's not. But you don't either and you never will.'

'I don't want to own her.'

'Don't you?' Sam shook his head. 'By taking Abbey

away from Sapphire Cove, what would she have but you? She'd be totally dependent on you for her happiness. And you? Would it be the same for you? Will you be dependent on her? I don't think so. I'll just bet you don't intend to drop your work commitments by one bit.'

'I can't. Dad—'

'So you won't change your lifestyle and you'll expect Abbey to fit in around the edges of your existing life?' Sam demanded harshly.

'Other women marry men like me.'

'Other women aren't Abbey,' Sam said roughly, and he sat heavily on the bed. 'If you want "other women" go marry "other women". If you want Abbey I suggest you marry her for what she is. A woman with a heart too big to ever think of leaving us.'

He looked up at his son and his eyes were full of pain.

'I'm feeling too tired to go look for turtle eggs,' he said sadly. 'You go by yourself. Stare out to sea and think about whether poverty really means peanuts! Or whether you really know what love means at all.'

CHAPTER TWELVE

THE following few days were some of the bleakest of Abbey's life.

She should have been cheerful. So many of her problems were solved.

Janet's walking went from strength to strength. At the end of the following week Janet could walk, unaided, from one end of the corridor to the other, and was agitating to go home. Only the knowledge that she'd refuse to take things easy when she did go home made Abbey keep her in hospital for a few days longer.

Sam was home already. Ryan had taken him out to the farm and Abbey hardly saw either of them.

'If there were problems we'd have heard,' Steve Pryor told her at the end of the following Friday. 'But, if you're worried, why don't you take off early and drop in and see him?'

'No.'

Abbey and Steve had been sharing the workload for the previous week and had found they worked well together. With two doctors working together, everything was well under control. The hospital was quiet and there was no reason Abbey shouldn't leave early. But to drop in on Sam meant dropping in on Ryan.

No and no and no.

'Are you busy tomorrow?' Steve asked, and Abbey hauled her thoughts back to work.

'No. I'm not busy and my babysitter's available if you want me to work.'

'Could you run the morning clinic?' Steve asked. Then he turned pink. 'I... Caroline and I...'

Caroline. The pretty young night sister.

Abbey smiled. 'You'd like to do something together?'

'Just spend the day at the beach,' Steve confessed. His blush deepened. 'I don't usually swim but Caroline…'

Caroline was hauling this young man from his academic pursuits with the strength of a bulldozer, Abbey thought. Steve only had a week more to work in Sapphire Cove but if Caroline had her way…

Her thoughts flew off at a tangent. Maybe Steve could be persuaded to work here. Then she could leave…

No, she couldn't. There was still Janet. There were still her debts. There was still her little son who should be brought up in the place his father loved.

'What's wrong, Abbey?' Steve asked gently. 'You look sad.'

'Do I?' Abbey managed a smile. 'Nope. I was just reminiscing about young love. Far be it from me to put my oar between the pair of you. Certainly have the day off with Caroline. You can work Sunday.'

'I hoped you'd say that.' Steve leaned over and kissed her on the nose. As working companions they'd achieved almost instant rapport and Abbey was growing fonder of this owlish young man by the minute. 'And I wouldn't get too nostalgic about young love just yet, Dr Wittner. You're not exactly grey-haired and matronly.'

'I'm a widow, Steve.'

'And Ryan Henry's just lost a fiancée.'

'Steve…'

'I know.' Steve held up his hands in mock surrender. 'You're just good friends. And I'm the monkey's uncle.'

He laughed and left her, walking down the hospital corridor with his stethoscope swinging jauntily and a bounce in his step.

Steve was in love and he wanted the world to be in love with him. Well, Abbey was in love, but…

But there was no happy ending for her love. It didn't put a bounce in her step.

A week from today Ryan was due to go back to New York, and life was due to go right back to where she'd left off three weeks ago.

There was no real need for her to even say goodbye, she thought bleakly. Ryan could leave next week without her seeing him again.

It didn't happen, of course.

Later that night Ryan telephoned her and asked if he could see her.

Abbey closed her eyes in pain, told him she was busy and put the phone down on its cradle before she broke down and wept.

She stayed awake all night and stared into the darkness. Thought about the impossibility of what Ryan was asking her to do. Thought about the impossibility of not doing what he wanted. Thought about life without Ryan.

Impossible.

On Saturday morning she rose and dressed, and the shadows on her face were darker than ever. She performed morning surgery like an automaton, and by the end of the morning there wasn't a patient she'd seen who didn't know there was something seriously amiss with Sapphire Cove's Dr Wittner.

And most of them figured what it was.

There were telephone calls going from one end of the community to the other. But the last telephone call of the morning was the worst. Abbey was in Sister's station when it came though.

It was Rod at the surf club, and his voice was shaking as he tried to speak.

'Dr Wittner, you'd better get over here fast. Some idiot's driven a jet ski straight through the stinger net and into the swimmers. We've got two children and Dr Pryor injured here—and they're all in a bad way.'

A jet ski.

Abbey stood motionless for two seconds while she took this on board and there was no comfort in her thoughts. Jet skis were like powerful motorbikes on water. They were

totally banned from the swimming beach. Dear heaven…
The injuries could be horrific.

'I'm on my way,' she snapped. 'Pressure on bleeding
wounds, Rod. You know. You can cope until I get there.'

She slammed down the phone and turned to Eileen.
Eileen had been pushing a medication trolley down the corridor but had stopped dead. She'd seen Abbey's face.

'Eileen, take over the phone,' Abbey told her, her mind
racing. 'Tell the ambulance to get to the surf club fast. A
jet ski's hit swimmers and there are three casualties. Rod
sounds horrified and he doesn't scare easily. I'm going
ahead now. Tell the boys to bring as much plasma as they
can find. If you can find someone to cover for you here
then you come too. Ring the air ambulance from Cairns
and get a helicopter here fast. And, Eileen?'

'Yes?'

Abbey took a deep breath. 'Ring Dr Henry. If he's still
in Sapphire Cove we need him. I have a feeling we need
everyone we can get.'

For the five minutes it took Abbey to reach the beach
she prayed she was overreacting. Surely calling the air ambulance was unnecessary. Surely notifying Ryan was stupid.

She wasn't overreacting at all.

Abbey's car flew over the last hill and one look at the
beach told her she was in dire trouble.

No one was in the water, and for a hot Saturday that was
almost unheard-of. Instead, there were scores of people
milling around the beach in horrified clusters.

There were three main groups. Two children had been
injured, Rob had said, and Dr Pryor. Steve…

Dear heaven.

Abbey pushed her little car as far over the beach as she
dared, then grabbed her bag and ran the rest of the way.
Her bruised knee was forgotten.

There were people everywhere!

'Abbey!' It was Rod, seeing her and calling through the

crowd, and his voice was urgent. 'Abbey, I need you here. Now!'

Not yet. First she should check all casualties and sort out priorities. Triage... Abbey gave a helpless look around. There seemed to be blood and people everywhere. Many of the swimmers were bloodstained. At a guess, many had carried the injured from the water.

There was mass shock, mass distress and tears, and the sobbing of frightened children.

Caroline, the nurse who'd come to the beach with Steve, was bending over a child, and she seemed to be working frantically. But Rod's voice was just as frantic and Abbey finally abandoned triage as an impossibility. She trusted Rod enough to be led. Two seconds later she was at Rod's side and she knew there could be no higher priority than the one facing her.

Steve.

Steve Pryor's leg was slashed to the bone and bright red arterial blood was spurting upwards.

'I can't stop it,' Rod gasped. 'Abbey, help.' He was searching desperately for a pressure point and getting nowhere. The wound was massive.

'Get me towels!' Abbey snatched the first towel she could see from one of the limp and appalled bystanders. She shoved it into a pad over Steve's leg and pressed as hard as she could. She used every muscle she had, and a few she didn't know she possessed, as she pressed downward.

'OK, Rod, wind another towel around the top of his leg. Fast. You'll have to burrow under the leg as I can't take the pressure off here. And, Don...' She looked up and directed her gaze at a middle-aged man with a beer gut. The local publican.

'Don, I need your help. Get everyone's towels, beachbags—anything you can lay your hands on—and shove them under Steve from his waist to his feet. Work under me. Put them under his hips, use them to shore up sand

and build a pile. I want Steve's legs to be above his heart from waist to ankles.'

The publican looked a sickly shade of green.

'Abbey, I can't...'

'Don't give me can't!' Abbey snapped. 'Steve'll die if you can't. Just do it!'

As the publican moved to do her bidding Abbey glanced up as another car roared across the beach and stopped in a shower of sand, its tyres spinning.

Ryan, too, had beaten the ambulance.

Ryan... She wasn't alone.

There was no time for Abbey to do more than glance upwards and say a tiny thankful prayer that Eileen had been able to locate him. All her concentration was on getting enough pressure on the pad to stop Steve bleeding.

Where on earth was the ambulance? She had to have plasma. Now!

And what about the injured children?

'Ryan, I haven't done triage,' she gasped as Ryan reached her side. She was pushing down as hard as she could on Steve's leg and she couldn't move. 'There are two others hurt but I can't leave this.'

'There's a girl with a gashed arm. My boys are dealing with her,' Rod told her briefly. He was hauling another towel tight around Steve's upper leg. He glanced up at Ryan. 'But Leith Kinley's just over there, Doc, and she's hurt bad. We carried her out of the water on a surfboard because she wasn't feeling her legs. Caroline—the nurse who was with Doc Pryor—is with her but she looks... I dunno...'

Leith Kinley... Their little asthmatic. Ryan's swimming pupil.

Ryan took one long, hard look down at the near-unconscious Steve and turned to where Leith was lying ten yards away. Abbey felt her heart give a sickening lurch. Leith... But she had to leave Leith to Ryan. If she didn't concentrate on what she was doing Steve would bleed to death under her hands.

Where on earth was the ambulance?

And what had happened? It seemed inconceivable that someone just ride a jet ski into the swimming beach.

And then the ambulance screamed across the sand, followed by the local police car, the fire truck and the State Emergency Services van for good measure. Eileen had clearly decided that the more people helping the better.

And Eileen herself arrived in the hospital car.

With plasma. Eileen had plasma.

For Steve, plasma meant the difference between life and death, and he'd lost so much blood now that the line between the two was growing very close indeed.

For the next few minutes Abbey couldn't think past getting the plasma running into Steve's body and the flood of blood from his leg completely stopped. Finally, with the combined effort of Abbey, Rod, Don and Eileen, they achieved success.

Abbey sat back in the sand and looked down. She took three deep breaths, as if she hadn't had time to breathe until now. Steve's leg was no longer bleeding. The tourniquet would have to be loosened every few minutes to let the blood flow through but she'd tied towelling pads across the wound so tightly that it shouldn't be a problem.

Plasma and intravenous fluids were flowing into Steve's veins. And adrenalin to counter shock. His pulse was thready but still there. He was young and strong. He'd need a decent surgeon to repair the damage to his thigh but, barring complications, Steve should live.

'You'll make it, Steve,' Abbey whispered as she saw his eyelids flutter open. She gripped his hand and held tight. She'd only known this young doctor for three weeks but he was already a friend.

'He's a bloody hero,' Don said faintly. Despite his initial protest, Don had worked like a Trojan, building Steve up with towels and sand so his thighs were at a thirty degree angle to his torso. It had made Abbey's job of stemming the blood loss much easier, and Don hadn't fainted once. Now, though, with urgent needs over, Don shoved his head between his knees and took a few deep breaths himself. When he finally raised his head he looked better.

'You know he saved the kids?' Don said.

'How?' Abbey was looping a vast strip of Elastoplast around the pad of towels pressing down on Steve's leg. She didn't want the pad coming loose before he reached Cairns. Steve would have to go to Cairns, she knew, and probably on to Brisbane. He needed plastic surgeons skilled in reconstruction for this leg.

'There was a bloody kid on a jet ski,' Don told her roughly, glaring around the beach as if trying to locate him. 'Showing off outside the nets. In bathers and no other protection, mind.

'Then the obvious happens. He gets stung by a stinger of some sort and assumes it's a box jellyfish. Panics and starts screaming and then comes haring through the nets to the beach. Forgot the nets would foul him. Got all tangled up and wrenched out of it—straight into a group of kids.

'Steve here saw him coming,' Don added, staring down at the injured doctor in awe. 'Faster than the rest of us put together, I reckon. He lunged across and shoved the kids out of the way. If it wasn't for Steve, it's my guess we'd have half a dozen dead kids.'

'Oh, Steve...'

'And then Caroline—the only qualified nurse on the beach—tried to stop his leg bleeding and Steve made her go to Leith,' Rod added. The lifesaver had fixed the tourniquet to his satisfaction and now was wiping some of the blood from his hands with an already bloodied towel.

Towel sales in Sapphire Cove were due to go through the roof in the next few days, Abbey thought grimly.

'Caroline showed us how to get Leith out of the water without moving her back but, meanwhile, Steve here was bleeding like a stuck pig.' The lifesaver shoved his hand on Steve's shoulder and gripped hard. 'You're all right, mate. A bloody hero.'

Bloody was right. No one smiled.

'Leith,' Steve said faintly. 'Abbey, Leith...'

'Ryan's with Leith,' Abbey told him.

'You go too... I'll be right. You go...'

Abbey stooped and gave him a quick hug, sent a silent message to Eileen with her eyes to look after him—and then went.

Once Steve's bleeding had stopped, Leith was in more trouble than Steve.

She was conscious and there seemed little blood, but as Abbey approached she could tell things were serious by the look of grimness around Ryan's mouth.

'Ryan?'

Ryan looked up and saw her and then looked down again. He was injecting morphine into Leith's lateral thigh and it took his entire attention.

He signalled to Caroline to keep holding the little girl's hands.

'That'll stop the pain, Leith,' Ryan said gently. 'Just don't move one inch. You hear? I want the painkillers to work and they can't work if you move.'

He rose to greet Abbey.

'Steve?' There was no disguising the anxiety in Ryan's voice.

'I've stopped the bleeding and I've set up a line for plasma. He should be OK.'

'The leg?'

'Retrievable. Not by me, though. I'd imagine he'll have to go to Brisbane. The air ambulance service is sending a helicopter. It should be here any minute. They'll take him to Cairns, stabilise him and send him on. Leith?'

'I'd guess fractured spine.'

'Oh, Ryan...'

'I'm not sure of the damage,' Ryan said grimly, 'but she's not feeling her legs. What else is there?'

'I'll find out,' Abbey said grimly. 'Oh, God...'

The other two casualties were a child with a gashed arm— it'd need stitching but Abbey could do that at Sapphire

Cove—and a boy with a bluebottle sting. The rider of the jet ski.

'I thought I must have been stung by a box jellyfish, like that boy was a couple of weeks back,' Paul muttered over and over again. Bluebottles were tiny air-filled sac-like jellyfish that trailed along the water's surface. They stung, but the pain eased after thirty minutes or so with no lasting damage. Paul was all of twelve years old and what had happened had him appalled. 'I never meant... I never...'

'It's not your fault, Paul,' Abbey said wearily, and she gave him a hug as she washed down his leg with fresh water. She was right. It was his stupid parents for letting him have such a powerful machine in the first place.

Abbey badly wanted to kick someone—and she couldn't kick a twelve-year-old. His parents were just as appalled as Paul. They were being punished enough, without Abbey kicking.

Which didn't ease Abbey's desire to kick one bit.

She went back to check Steve and found him drifting in and out of consciousness. She'd given him as much morphine as she dared.

And then the helicopter roared in overhead and came in to land on the firm, damp sand at the water's edge.

'You go with them,' Abbey yelled at Ryan over the noise of the chopper as Steve and Leith were skilfully loaded onto stretchers. She glanced down at Leith and her mouth tightened in fear. A broken back. Was Leith facing paraplegia—or worse? Maybe...maybe with Ryan the child had a chance. Spinal injuries were so unpredictable. But if Ryan was there...

'Please, Ryan. I want you to go.'

Ryan looked down at Abbey with an unreadable expression on his face.

And he went.

CHAPTER THIRTEEN

RYAN was away for five days.

For those five days Abbey hardly had time to blink. She was thrust back into her old workload with a vengeance.

Steve Pryor was undergoing massive reconstruction of his thigh. He wouldn't lose his leg, but it would take months before he was able to use it in anywhere near a normal fashion.

Caroline, the night sister who'd spent the day at the beach with him, travelled to Brisbane so there'd be someone with him during major surgery. It turned out Steve had no family. Caroline was it. And, by the look of her haggard face as she arrived back in Sapphire Cove, Abbey knew Caroline wouldn't have it any other way.

'He's such an owl,' Caroline sniffed into Abbey's arms. 'Such a gentle, loving person. And he saved those kids. I don't think I can bear it.'

'You're in love with him,' Abbey said on a note of discovery, and that produced more sniffs and a fast retreat into a handkerchief.

'Yes, but now... I mean it all happened so fast. I only went out with him the once and how's he supposed to believe I love him already? And now he's in Brisbane and I'm here and he was only here on a locum anyway and I'm never going to see him again.'

'Let's see what Steve has to say about that when he's feeling a bit better.' Abbey smiled. And then asked what she most wanted to know. 'Now, tell me. How's Leith? Is Ryan still with her?'

Caroline hauled herself together and blew her nose. And managed a watery smile.

'Dr Henry assisted at the operation. The surgeons down there asked him to. Oh, Dr Wittner, they think he's wonderful. No one thought she'd walk again but there's some new technique Dr Henry knew was being trialled.

'The surgeons here did a video conferencing session with some of Dr Henry's colleagues in the States—paediatric orthopaedic surgeons, the best in the world. Dr Henry organised it so it seemed like they were actually in the theatre while they were operating on Abbey. And now they say there's a really good chance she will walk.'

Well, well.

Abbey took it all in and hugged it against her heart. It helped. It helped that even if she couldn't marry Ryan the Ryan she knew and loved was still going strong.

She was proud of him. She ached for him. She loved him.

It had to be shoved aside for the moment. There'd be time to be really miserable later. There were all sorts of after-effects from the accident on the beach. Paul, the child who'd been riding the jet ski, had been admitted to hospital, suffering from shock, and it would take all her skills to pull him out of it without serious emotional scars. His parents were almost as bad. Basically good-hearted people, they were deeply distressed at what had happened.

The police sergeant wasn't helping. He wanted blood, and when Abbey counselled him strongly about taking it further he broke down and wept and needed help himself.

The small child with the gashed arm was the least of her worries. Wendy was proud of her stitches but her parents were upset. Then the local school teacher wanted Abbey to come and speak to the children at assembly as the children were desperate to know what was going on.

And there was her ordinary hospital work. Abbey asked the farmers to take over her cows again and Marcia kept on helping with Jack, but still she finished each day exhausted. And missing Ryan.

Janet was still recovering, following her exercise regime with stoic determination. With reason.

On the fifth day after the accident Abbey walked into Janet's ward to find her sitting up in bed with Sam at her side. That didn't surprise her. Sam had been a constant visitor. What did surprise her were the silly grins on both of their faces. They sat hand in hand on the bed and they looked for all the world like two teenagers caught having an illicit cuddle.

Abbey lifted her eyebrows and smiled a query.

'Sorry, guys. You want me to come back later?'

'No.' Janet blushed and looked at Sam. And blushed again.

'We have something to say to you,' Sam said seriously. And it was his turn to turn pink.

And Abbey knew.

'You want to ask for Janet's hand in marriage,' she said in delight. 'Don't you?'

'Well…' Sam's smile deepened in quiet satisfaction. 'I should ask someone.'

'Have you asked Janet?'

'Yes.'

'And she said?'

'Yes,' Sam said bluntly. 'She said she'll marry me if you'll marry Ryan.'

Abbey frowned. 'I like the marriage idea,' she said slowly. 'I don't agree with the *if* part of the deal. It doesn't make sense.'

'That's what I told her,' Sam said, 'but she won't leave you by yourself.'

'I'm not by myself.' Abbey took a deep breath. 'So…you two love each other?'

'Yes,' Sam said firmly, and put his arm around Janet's waist. 'We do.'

'Then I'm walking out of here right now and announcing it to the world,' Abbey told them. 'Sam and Janet are getting married. And there's no conditions applying. Not one!'

She hugged them both. 'And don't you dare stuff this up by stupid quibbles, Janet Wittner,' she ordered. 'You've got your Sam. And I have my little Jack. I won't be lonely.'

Only it wasn't quite true. Jack was here, but anywhere without Ryan was lonely.

Where was he? He'd been away for five days. Why didn't he return?

Half of her was starting to think that the next thing they'd hear from Ryan would be a phone call from New York to say that his career had reclaimed him, and it was time to get on with his life.

At two the next morning someone knocked hard on Abbey's door.

Abbey flicked on her bedside light and looked blearily at the clock. Two?

People telephoned in an emergency. They didn't come here.

For a moment she felt a pang of alarm. This little cottage was set back far from the road and, apart from Jack, she was alone. Still, if it was an emergency...

She hauled a wrap around her flimsy nightgown, went to the door and opened it a crack.

Ryan.

She shut it again. For the life of her, she couldn't think of anything else to do.

'Abbey!'

'Go away, Ryan Henry,' she said breathlessly. 'It's two in the morning. I'm not...I'm not dressed to receive visitors.'

'I'm not a visitor. I'm me.'

'Ryan...'

'Twenty years ago, when I came at midnight to take you turtle-hunting, you never had maidenly quibbles.'

'You want to go turtle-hunting?' she demanded with her back to the door, and Ryan laughed.

'No, Abbey, I don't. I'm looking for something much more precious. Let me in.'

'Why should I?'

'Because I love you.'

Silence.

The words echoed round and round Abbey's little living room.

This was dangerous.

'Ryan...'

'Abbey, I'm not here to demand you leave everything you love,' Ryan pleaded. 'I promise. Let me in.'

Abbey took a deep breath. This was mad. Crazy. But there was nothing else to do but let him in.

She'd expected to open the door and have him sedately step inside. No such thing. She opened the door an inch, it was shoved wide with ruthless force and she was swept right up into Ryan's arms and kissed so thoroughly that there was no possible way she could protest.

And after the first millisecond she didn't try.

Abbey wound her arms around his neck and kissed him right back.

Crazy, crazy, crazy.

But sense was for tomorrow. Crazy was for now.

Ryan was for now.

He swung her round and round the room, his kiss intensifying as he whirled. Abbey was laughing and dizzy and so madly in love her feet wouldn't have touched the ground even if she'd been standing.

There was only Ryan. There was only this love.

And finally—somehow—they were in her bedroom, falling onto the soft covers. And Ryan's mouth left off claiming hers. He lay with Abbey in his arms and he pulled away so he could see her. His hand reached up and switched off the bedlight and there was only the light from the full moon, glimmering onto the land and through the open window from the sea.

'Woman, you are driving me crazy,' Ryan groaned. 'You know that? Five days... Five days since I've seen you and I haven't had you out of my head for one minute. Abbey, you must marry me. To save my sanity, you must...' And he hauled her tighter to him, tighter—until his need was her need and the world was fusing in a mist of love and desire and the coming together of two people who were right for each other.

But they weren't. They couldn't be.

Somehow Abbey made herself push away. She held Ryan at arm's length and she looked into his eyes in the dim light. And what she saw there told her that she was truly loved.

But it wasn't enough.

In the next bedroom lay her little boy. And there was a hospital five minutes down the road that depended on her. And Janet?

No. Janet had sorted out her own loneliness. But there was no way Abbey could find the same happiness.

'Ryan, this is crazy. We can't...' Her breath broke on a sob. 'I can't...'

'You can.' Ryan's hand held her and he smiled—a smile that made her heart do crazy things inside her breast. 'Abbey, for the past five days I've been thinking. Really thinking. Leith's injury...'

'Leith...'

'It's touch and go whether she'll walk again.' Ryan told her. 'She needs expert rehabilitation. More than just swimming lessons now. And I thought, if I went back to the States I'd never know that it was done properly. I'd walk away and it would be up to others to see that she had the right treatment.'

'But—'

'Hush,' he told her. 'Listen. Over the past five days, I've been seeing Sapphire Cove at its best. I've watched how surrounded Leith's parents have been.

'And Steve... He's down there in Brisbane and he has no family at all but I don't think there's a family in Sapphire Cove who haven't sent him flowers or chocolates or fruit or something! The local primary-school children have sent him pictures to decorate his walls. His bedroom's packed, he's touched to the core and he wants to come back.

'Steve's been a loner all his life, trying to find roots, and he's found them here. He wants to work here.'

'What—permanently?'

'Yes. He wants to marry Caroline and stay here.'

'Are you saying I could go because of that?' Abbey asked slowly. 'Go with you? To the States?'

'No.' He kissed her then, lightly, on the nose. 'I'm not. At first that's what I thought but then...the more I thought about it the more jealous I grew. Jealous of Steve. His decision seemed so right. To stay here with the woman he loved. To live long term in a community like this. To bring his kids up where they could hunt for turtles.'

'S-so?'

'So, if it's OK with you, I'll rearrange my life,' Ryan said seriously. 'Steve and I have it figured.'

'Steve and you...'

'Steve and I. And my co-researchers in the States. The reason I've come here so late is that this is the only reasonable time I can talk to New York and I've been trying to organise everything so I can hand you a deal on a platter.' He hauled her close again and kissed her.

'A deal, Abbey Rhodes. Abbey Wittner. Abbey soon-to-be-Henry. You want to hear my deal? It's taken me days and days to organise it so it's worth a listen.'

And he kissed her again, so deeply that there was no way in the wide world that she could hear anything at all.

Then he managed to pull away. Ryan was laughing down at her in the moonlight, triumphant and loving. And Abbey's heart was turning somersault after somersault, so fast she could hardly breathe.

'Want to hear?' he demanded again, and Abbey managed a shaken laugh.

'Oh, Ryan, of course I want to hear. Of course.'

'My plan is this.' He held her at arm's length and groaned. 'Hell, Abbey, stop looking so damned beautiful. I can't make myself think here.'

'Think,' she told him severely. 'You need a bucket of cold water, Ryan Henry.' Then she reached out and touched him on the lips with her finger. And laughed with joy. 'I need a bucket of cold water myself. Tell me fast, Ryan,' she begged. 'Fast.'

'I'm moving here to live. Permanently.'

That stopped her. The laughter died.

'Ryan, you can't,' she said uncertainly. 'Your career...' She shook her head. 'Ryan, you'd be like me in the States. A fish out of water.'

'Nope.' He pulled her to him again and kissed her hair. 'Not a fish out of water.' He held her close and spoke thickly into her curls. 'It's all organised. Steve's interested in my research areas. He's bright and young and keen as mustard. Cairns is only an hour and a half away and it has an international airport. We're going to keep on with our research. I'm going to keep on with my teaching commitments in the States—via video conferencing.

'I'll be working here with Steve, intermittently in Cairns and Brisbane, and twice a year I'll have to fly back to the States for two-week stints at the hospital where I'm based now. But ninety per cent of the time I'll be based here, Abbey Wittner. Here!'

'But...but how?'

'The world is getting smaller,' Ryan told her, holding her close. 'With video conferencing, the Internet, e-mail—hell, Abbey, I spend my life in the States on the end of a modem, talking to doctors two rooms away. Now I'll be doing the same thing but I'll be half a world away.

'And I'll keep my feet on the ground by indulging in a little general practice. As will Steve. So, between us, we'll give Sapphire Cove three part-time doctors. You and me and Steve. And we'll all live happily ever after.'

Then the laughter in his voice died and his eyes became a trace uncertain. Anxious. 'How does that sound, my lovely Abbey? Will it work? Will you mind me going back to the States—leaving you for two weeks twice a year? I'll give up my research if I must—to win you. If it's not enough.'

'Oh, Ryan...'

'Tell me, Abbey.'

'No,' Abbey said breathlessly, and her eyes were bright with unshed tears. 'It's not enough, Ryan Henry. Eleven months of a year are not enough as a basis for a marriage...'

'Abbey...'

'I'll only marry you on one condition, Ryan Henry,' Abbey murmured joyfully, and she put her arms around him and held him close. So close she thought she'd never let him go again. Not ever.

'Condition?' Ryan's voice was slurred by love and desire. Abbey's body was curled into his and his hands were sliding under her wrap. Feeling the delicious contours of her body. Pulling her against him.

A man and a woman, becoming one.

'On condition that when you go back to the States for your month every year I'm going too,' Abbey told him. 'Me and Jack. Your family. Whither thou goest, I go, my love. My home is your home, Ryan Henry. My heart is your heart.'

Ryan closed his eyes. In any man's life there should be this pinnacle of joy, he told himself. This was it. This was the moment he'd been waiting for all his life, and now he was here he couldn't believe he'd reached it.

'You want to wake Jack?' he asked, and his voice was as unsteady as he'd ever heard it. As unsure. 'Tell him he's got a new daddy?'

But Abbey was shaking her head and her hands were moving down...down... In a gesture of pure wifely possession.

'Let's not,' she whispered as her fingers found what they were looking for.

'Let's do something else.'

CHAPTER FOURTEEN

RYAN and Abbey Henry's honeymoon lasted one whole night before it was interrupted.

Janet and Sam, married two weeks earlier—'we're in our seventies: we don't have as much time as you young things for wasting time unmarried'—were caring for Jack. Steve, walking with a limp but well on the way to recovery, was caring for the hospital. Two weeks of 'Bliss'...

The discussion on where to go had been short.

'You hijacked one honeymoon of mine at "Bliss",' Ryan told Abbey severely. 'It's your duty to give me another.'

And Abbey couldn't think of a single reason to disagree.

On the first morning of her honeymoon Abbey woke late, stirred and found she was going nowhere. She was being held fast in Ryan's arms. Ryan felt her wake. He shifted slightly so he could look down at her.

His wife.

His lovely, lovely Abbey.

The wedding had been perfect. The tiny church high on the headland overlooking Sapphire Cove... Everyone there...

Last night had been perfect. The merging of two bodies into one.

Abbey. His wife.

Ryan's arms pulled her closer as the knowledge of Abbey as his bride—his woman for always—surged though him.

And then the phone rang. Of course the phone rang. The medical imperative!

'If that's an earthquake I don't want to know about it,' Abbey murmured sleepily, snuggling in closer against her love. But there was a sinking sensation in the pit of her stomach all the same. No one would disturb them unless it was an emergency, and one thing Abbey didn't want for the rest of her life was emergencies.

It was a pity, then, that she was a doctor.

Ryan sighed and lifted the receiver. 'Ryan Henry.' Abbey could tell by the sound of his voice that he was as tense as she was.

But then Ryan smiled as he listened to the disembodied voice on the end of the line. When the voice had finished speaking he put the phone down.

'Come on, my love,' Ryan said, and he lifted Abbey into his arms and kissed her soundly. 'Time to get ourselves decent. The honeymoon's on hold for an hour or two.'

'Oh, Ryan…' It was a wail of dismay. Medical imperatives be damned, Abbey thought bitterly. She wanted this time alone with her love.

And then she looked more closely at Ryan's face. His smile was growing.

'What is it?' she asked.

'I'm not missing this, even for a honeymoon,' Ryan told her, swinging his legs over the edge of the bed and reaching for his pants. 'Come on, Abbey. Let's go. Our turtles are hatching.'

The entire population of Sapphire Cove was on the beach.

There was no way anyone could have predicted exactly when the turtles would hatch. The experts said between fifty-four and seventy days, depending on the depth they were buried and the strength of the sun. So, apart from setting up a duty roster of guards, no one had planned for this.

But everyone was here. Abbey looked around in amazement as she and Ryan pulled to a halt. Everyone!

School had been let out. Grandmas and grandpas were arriving in convoys. The local shopkeepers and bankers and publicans had closed shop and headed for the beach.

Steve and Caroline stood hand in hand by the water's edge, Steve leaning lightly on Caroline's arm to support his weak leg.

There were men and women in wheelchairs and with walking sticks, and even a couple of stretcher cases being carried by volunteers. The hospital inmates had come *en masse*. Here were patients who were too sick to walk, but who wouldn't miss this for the world.

Ted was here, holding a small child from Children's ward and trying hard to keep his expression ghoulish when really he was as filled with wonder as everyone else.

Who else?

Ian Miller was here, dressed in the neat trousers and tie that denoted the professional. Sapphire Cove's newest solicitor was taking his first holiday. Ian's grin was as broad as his face, and his mother beside him had a matching smile a mile wide.

Leith Kinley was here, confined to a wheelchair but only just. Four days ago she'd stood for the first time. She'd be going back to Brisbane soon for more intensive rehabilitation but she'd been allowed home for Abbey's and Ryan's wedding.

And now she was here for this. Sapphire Cove's event of the decade.

There were two long lines of people, forming an avenue of honour from the freshly scattered mound where the turtle had laid her eggs down to the sea.

An avenue of honour for the hatchlings.

One by one they came. Tiny, tiny turtles, wide-eyed and terrified, scrambling through the sand, burrowing their way out into the open, blinking in the sunlight—and then heading for the sea.

Up above were their enemies. Gulls and terns and all sorts of seabirds, wheeling and squawking and demanding in no uncertain terms that these people depart and let them at their prey.

No way.

The school children were taking turns to toss bread further down the beach, filling the birds' stomachs and distracting them from tastier prey.

All along the line of honour umbrellas were being shaken

upwards. Umbrellas… Scores and scores of them in every colour of the rainbow, covering the tiny turtles' flight and preventing any daring gull from getting near.

And one by one the turtles were reaching the waves, stopping momentarily in shock at the first touch of foam— and then charging gamely on. Each one was two tiny inches of turtle, heading for the horizon.

Sapphire Cove couldn't protect these little ones once they reached the sea, but once there they had a chance. A chance of one day being as huge as their mother and returning here years hence to breed themselves.

Abbey and Ryan climbed from the car and stood on the grass verge, looking down at the spectacle before them.

Jack, safely held between Janet and Sam, saw his mother and crowed with delight—and then went right back to crowing with delight at the turtles.

Abbey's eyes filled with tears.

'Did you ever see such a sight?' she whispered to Ryan. 'Our turtles. Oh, Ryan, it's a miracle.'

'It is indeed a miracle,' Ryan agreed softly, his arm firmly around Abbey's waist and his eyes moving from the turtles to his brand new son—and then back to his wife.

And he held her close and kissed her, and kissed her again.

'Life is,' he said.

Life is a miracle.

MILLS & BOON®

Medical Romance™

COMING NEXT MONTH

TOMORROW'S CHILD by Lilian Darcy

A new start for Dr Paula Nichols and a new romance...

COUNTRY REMEDY by Joanna Neil

Why was Ross *so* appealing? And just when Heather had decided not to get involved!

CONTRACT DAD by Helen Shelton

Drew wasn't looking for a wife, Lizzy didn't want a husband—but she *did* want a baby!

A FAMILY TO SHARE by Gill Sanderson

Loving Sisters trilogy

LOVING SISTERS

Lisa Grey was a successful, extremely caring and stunning redhead. Just like her sisters, Emily and Rosalind, she had a lot to give but had yet to find the perfect partner. This first book tells how she met that man and how she fought to keep him. Coming soon are **A FAMILY AGAIN**, Emily's story, and **THE FAMILY FRIEND**, Rosalind's tale.

On sale from **11th September 1998**

Available at most branches of WH Smith, John Menzies, Martins, Tesco, Volume One and Safeway

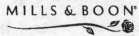

EMILIE RICHARDS

THE WAY BACK HOME

As a teenager, Anna Fitzgerald fled an impossible
situation, only to discover that life on the streets was
worse. But she had survived. Now, as a woman,
she lived with the constant threat that the secrets of
her past would eventually destroy her new life.

1-55166-399-6
AVAILABLE IN PAPERBACK
FROM SEPTEMBER, 1998

JASMINE CRESSWELL

THE DAUGHTER

Maggie Slade's been on the run for seven years now.
Seven years of living without a life or a future because
she's a woman with a past. And then she meets Sean
McLeod. Maggie has two choices. She can either run,
or learn to trust again and prove her innocence.

"Romantic suspense at its finest."

—Affaire de Coeur

1-55166-425-9
**AVAILABLE IN PAPERBACK
FROM SEPTEMBER, 1998**

DEBBIE MACOMBER

Married in Montana

Needing a safe place for her sons to grow up, Molly
Cogan decided it was time to return home.
Home to Sweetgrass Montana.
Home to her grandfather's ranch.

*"Debbie Macomber's name on a book is a guarantee
of delightful, warm-hearted romance."*
—Jayne Ann Krentz

MIRA®

1-55166-400-3
**AVAILABLE IN PAPERBACK
FROM AUGUST, 1998**

WORD LINK

We are giving away a year's supply of Mills & Boon® books to the five lucky winners of our latest competition. Simply fill in the ten missing words below, complete the coupon overleaf and send this entire page to us by 28th February 1999. The first five correct entries will each win a year's subscription to the Mills & Boon series of their choice. What could be easier?

BUSINESS	**SUIT**	CASE
BOTTLE		HAT
FRONT		BELL
PARTY		BOX
SHOE		PIPE
RAIN		TIE
ARM		MAN
SIDE		ROOM
BEACH		GOWN
FOOT		KIND
BIRTHDAY		BOARD

Please turn over for details of how to enter ⇨

C8H

HOW TO ENTER

There are ten words missing from our list overleaf. Each of the missing words must link up with the two on either side to make a new word or words.

For example, 'Business' links with 'Suit' and 'Case' to form 'Business Suit' and 'Suit Case':

BUSINESS—SUIT—CASE

As you find each one, write it in the space provided. When you have linked up all the words, fill in the coupon below, pop this page into an envelope and post it today. Don't forget you could win a year's supply of Mills & Boon® books—you don't even need to pay for a stamp!

Mills & Boon Word Link Competition
FREEPOST CN81, Croydon, Surrey, CR9 3WZ

EIRE readers: (please affix stamp) PO Box 4546, Dublin 24.

Please tick the series you would like to receive if you are one of the lucky winners

Presents™ ❏ Enchanted™ ❏ Medical Romance™ ❏
Historical Romance™ ❏ Temptation®

Are you a Reader Service™ subscriber?   Yes ❏   No ❏

Ms/Mrs/Miss/Mr ....Initials.........................
                                          (BLOCK CAPITALS PLEASE)
Surname...

Address ....

....

....Postcode.........................

(I am over 18 years of age)   C8H